Material Girl 3: Secrets & Betrayals

By Keisha R. Ervin

1

Author Contact Info

keisha_ervin2002@yahoo.com

askkeishaandmo@yahoo.com

www.facebook.com/keisha.ervin

www.twitter.com/keishaervin

Instagram: keishaervin

www.youtube.com/user/ColorMePynk

www.prettyratchetthingz.com

2

Table of Content

<u>Dedication</u>

After unexpectedly becoming sick in 2012, I took a
year and half off to concentrate on my health and figure out
who I was. Throughout that time you, my supporters stood
by my side. You all encouraged me, prayed for me, laughed
with me and waited patiently for my return to the literary
world. I can't say thank you enough. You all have truly
blessed my life. I am a better woman because of your
consistent love and support so I dedicate this long-awaited
novel to you...

Acknowledgments

Lord, I wanna say thank you!!! Thank you for keeping me wrapped in your arms when the world seemed too cold and unbearable. You are my savior, my friend and confidant. With you Lord, I share my deepest darkest secrets, my desires, my fears and my dreams. Without you I wouldn't have made it through one of the most trying times of my life. You're love kept me sane. You have shown me what it means to truly believe in your word and how when you do, you are blessed for it. Thank you for giving me a new outlook on life. Lord, know that I will continue to praise your name. I love you, Lord.

To my angel on earth, Kyrese. You are the love of my life. Without you, there is no me. You're the Clyde to my Bonnie. When I started in this literary game eleven years ago, you were just four years old. Fast forward eleven years later and now you are fourteen years old and about to start high school. My, how times flies. You are becoming a young man and I'm proud to say that you are my son. God blessing me with you is the greatest gift I have and will ever receive.

Daddy, I love you to infinity and beyond. Thank you for stepping up and being the father that I have always prayed for. I'm so happy that you and I have become as close as we are now. I will forever be your, Fat Mama.

Mama, girl, smh. I love you like a fat kid loves cake, like Ike loved to beat Tina, like Diddy liked to wear shiny suits. You are the best mother that a girl could ask for, muah!

To 3LB aka 3 Little Bitches, Locia, Sharissa and Mo. Ya'll are not just my friends but you are my sisters. We are a family. If I didn't have you ladies in my life, I would be lost. When I'm sad, angry, curious, concerned, irked, happy or stressed out you all are there. Thank you for encouraging me, loving me, praying for me, laughing with me, singing with me, dancing with me, cracking jokes with me, doing business with me and most of all thank you for being my friend.

Miesha, you are my sister in Christ. On those late nights when I call you in need of the word, you are always there. I thank god for blessing me with you and my nieces and nephews. You are not only the best sister but the best hairstylist in the world.

Last but certainly not least, Brenda Hampton, words can't express how much of a blessing you have to been to my life. You're my second mother, my agent and friend. I love you and I can't wait to see where the next chapter of my life takes us.

They say that what goes up must come down but don't let me fall.
-B.o.B, "Don't Let Me Fall"

Chapter 1

"But it was just a dream, just a moment ago. I was up so high, lookin' down at the sky, don't let me fall," Dylan sang B.o.B's hit song while gazing happily down at her left hand. The ten carat emerald cut diamond ring by Harry Winston was so icy it almost blinded her eyesight. This was the moment in life that Musiq, Cee Lo Green, and Kindred the Family Soul sang about. Nothing else in life mattered but the sheer bliss that filled her soul.

Everything in her life was cool; she had a perfectly healthy happy baby boy who she loved more then life itself, two best friends that loved her unconditionally, she and her mother were on good terms, and after all the drama she'd gone through the past two years, she was now married to the love of her life.

Ecstatic about her decision, she sat Indian-style on top of a king size bed inside the Bellagio hotel. The Bellagio hotel was one of the premiere hotels in Las Vegas. It had been around for years. Icon's such as Frank Sinatra and Sammy Davis Jr. often frequented the hotel when alive and the box office hit Ocean's Eleven movie was filmed there.

Still dressed in her Vera Wang wedding gown, Dylan unfolded her legs and watched as Angel, her husband, popped open a bottle of Dom. With the bottle open, he poured them both a glass of champagne then headed towards Dylan. Layers of white crinoline surrounded her. She looked like a princess. Angel couldn't have been happier to call her his wife.

And yes the circumstance of how they became one was like a plotline from the soap opera General Hospital but he didn't care. Dylan was his. He'd known it from the moment they met.

"Here." He handed her a glass.

"Thanks hubby," Dylan smiled, gleefully.

"You wanna make a toast?"

"Mmm hmm," Dylan nodded her head.

"To me and you being together forever." Angel clicked his glass against hers, then gulped the entire drink down.

"Mmm that's good." Dylan relished the taste.

"So when am I going to be able to make love to my wife?" Angel ran his hand up her leg.

11

"Would that be me?" Dylan pointed to her chest, coyly.

"Who else would it be?" Angel stood up and unzipped his jeans.

Grinning from ear to ear Dylan lay back in anticipation of him entering her. She never wanted this moment to end. So much joy filled her heart she felt as if she was going to explode. But the fear of what was in store for her when she returned home kept nagging at her spirit. She'd left a shit load of drama back in the Lou.

Earlier that day Dylan left her fiancé of only a month, Javier Cruz, at the altar. Without any real explanation, she lifted up her dress and ran out of the church in search of the man who held her heart in the palm of his hand. After a thirty-minute ride, she found Angel at the airport going through security. Dylan hadn't cared that she might look like a deranged fool.

All she cared about was finding her man. It hadn't even gone through her mind that once she found him he might not want to have anything to do with her. She wasn't going to leave without Angel. Right there in the center of the airport Dylan professed her undying love for Angel in front of a crowd of people.

12

Overjoyed by her confession, Angel took her into his arms and assured that his love for her hadn't waivered or faded. From there they booked a private plane to Vegas. During the flight, Angel wasted no time proposing to Dylan. He'd had the ring for months. Not wanting to spend another second of her life without him she said yes. When they reached Vegas, the two immediately went to the Little White Chapel were numerous celebs like Britney Spears had gotten hitched.

Ten minutes later, they were husband and wife. Now here they were making love like it was their last moment on earth. Yes, Dylan had a lot of loose ends to tie up when her foot hit St. Louis soil but for now she was going to bask in the essence of being Mrs. Angel Carter.

Dylan had only been back in town a couple of hours but she had to see her girls Billie and Tee-Tee. She and Billie had been friends since as far as back as she could remember. Over the years, they'd become more than friends. Billie was like the sister she never had and because she'd married her brother, they were now legally sisters.

Billie had it going on. She was thirty-five years old with three children and a husband that made women want to drop their panties for. Billie was a go getter. She'd been raised by the motto where there is a will there is a way. Billie's drive and motivation was one of the things Dylan loved and despised about her. Billie often let her hard work and good deeds over shadow her own happiness.

Then there was Teyana aka Tee-Tee aka Thug Misses. Tee-Tee was Dylan's flamboyant over the top cousin. Dylan loved him dearly. Whether she wanted his opinion or not, Tee-Tee was always there to drop jewels. Tee-Tee was a personal shopper for Nordstrom and was married to a thug named Bernard and had a beautiful adopted daughter who they named Princess Gaga to everyone's chagrin. But nonetheless, she loved her cousin despite his crazy antics and over-the-top attitude.

Dylan pulled the entrance door to The Coffee Garden which was located around the corner from her house and walked in. It was mid-afternoon so the restaurant was crammed with people eating lunch. With her Chanel bag securely placed in the crook of her right arm, she sashayed towards the table where her best friend and cousin were sitting.

"What up bitches?!" She spoke cheerfully.

"Well, look at what the cat dragged in." Tee-Tee looked over his shoulder at her, pursing his lips.

Dylan kissed him on the cheek.

"Good afternoon to you too Tee-Tee," Dylan rolled her eyes.

"Bitch please," he frowned. "Don't try to sweet talk me. Where in the hell have you been? We have been worried sick about you. Hell, Mason done started calling me mama."

"Don't make me slap you," Dylan side-eyed Tee-Tee while air kissing each of Billie's cheeks.

"Don't get mad at me 'cause you one step away from becoming a Teen Mom."

"Any-who." Dylan waved him off. "You haters notice anything different about me?" She batted her eyes and posed like a mannequin.

"Please don't tell me you're pregnant again. 'Cause you lookin' mighty chunky around the middle." Tee-Tee pointed his index finger.

"You better be glad it ain't no knives on this table 'cause if there was I'd stab you." Dylan curled her upper lip. "Now guess!" She stomped her foot.

"You got butt injections? 'Cause you know that's all the rave now," Tee-Tee quizzed.

"No," Billie interjected, eyeing her quizzically. "She did something different with her hair."

15

"Actually, I did." Dylan ran her hand down the back of her head.

She was absolutely obsessed with her new pixie cut hairstyle.

"But that's not it. Angel and I got married!"

"You lyin'?" Billie said flabbergasted.

"Nope." Dylan extended her left hand.

"Ohhhhh Dylan," Billie's eyes filled with tears. "I'm so happy for you." She stood up and gave Dylan a warm hug.

"Thanks sis," Dylan gushed.

"We are sisters now aren't we?" Billie smiled back.

"Ya'll so fake." Tee-Tee said dryly with his arms folded across his chest.

"Eww what's wrong wit' you?" Dylan finally sat down.

"You just love to rain on my parade don't you?" Tee-Tee rolled his neck. "You know I let you slide when you got pregnant by Angel but now you have taken this shit way too far. Do you know it is taking everything in me not to jump across this table and … whoop … yo' … muthafuckin' … ass. Angel is my man, jumpoff!"

"Tee-Tee shut up!" Billie flicked her wrist.

"I just don't know where we gon' go from here."
Tee-Tee dabbed his eyes pretending to cry.

"Girl, ain't nobody got time for him," Dylan said.

"I agree. Now tell me everything." Billie said,
excited.

"Well, after I raced out of church like a mad
woman, I had the limousine driver take me to Lambert
Airport and once I got there I found Angel and professed
my love to him right there in front of everyone. I mean
folks were lookin' at me like I was out of my goddamn
mind but ask me if I give a fuck." Dylan pursed her lips.

"All I knew was I had to get my man back and
when your brother told me that he still loved me too it was
like God had kissed me on the forehead and said see baby I
told you everything is gonna be okay."

"Aww, Dylan." Billie poked out her bottom lip.

"After that we chartered a G5 to Vegas and got
married. Now I'm here with you guys," Dylan beamed.

"Fairytales do come true." Billie picked up her
glass.

Tee-Tee paced his index finger inside his mouth and
pretended to gag.

"Bye Fa'Jealous." Dylan waved her hand, flashing
her ring.

17

"Honey please. I'm far from jealous. If anybody's happy for you you know it's me. You know I love you like a sister or better yet a Birken bag." Tee-Tee reached his hand across the table and placed his hand on top of hers.

"Seriously, you and Angel are meant for each other. And I'm happy your family is finally complete."

"Thanks cousin." Dylan choked up.

"I know you ain't being no soft ass nigga," Tee-Tee insisted. "We some OG's and OG's don't cry."

"Shut up." Dylan giggled, gathering her emotions.

"Now, the million dollar question is, have you talked to your fiancé?" Tee-Tee arched his eyebrow.

"No." Dylan shook her head.

"Well, don't you think you need to?" Billie said.

"I am. I just don't know what to say to him." Dylan replied, feeling overwhelmed.

"Yeah, that is an awkward conversation to have." Billie took a sip from her cup.

"I said I was gonna go by his hotel room today after we have lunch and see if he was still there."

"Good luck wit' that girlfriend. I wouldn't want to be in your shoes. Even though they are some fabulous Manolo's," Tee-Tee admired her heels. "When we get those?"

"Angel bought them for me while we were in Vegas," Dylan gushed. "I swear ya'll I love that man. I can't wait to get back home. 'Cause as soon as I see him I'ma attack that dick like I'm the crocodile hunter."

After all the boys that I thought I loved before. I didn't know what love was until you knocked on my door.

-Keri Hilson, "All the Boys"

Chapter 2

A million butterflies fluttered around in the pit of Dylan's stomach as she knocked on Cruz's hotel door. A part of her prayed that he wouldn't answer and she wouldn't have to deal with the mess she'd made. But she had to make things right between them or else she would forever be tortured by the look on his face when she left him standing at the altar. To her dismay, after she knocked the second time, she heard the sound of his footsteps coming towards the door.

"Who is it?" He asked.

"It's me, Dylan." She spoke hesitantly.

"Who?" Cruz asked, surprised.

Cruz prayed that someone wasn't playing a cruel joke on him. His heart wouldn't be able to take it.

"Dylan," she repeated.

Overjoyed Cruz swung open the door in anticipation of seeing her face.

"Yo! Where have you been? I've been worried sick about you?" He pulled her into his arms and held her so tight she could hardy breathe.

"Oh." Dylan said caught off guard by his eagerness to see her.

She naturally assumed that Cruz would be livid with her and want to rip her head off.

"Let me look at you." He held her at arms length. "Are you okay?"

"Yes, I'm fine."

"Why haven't you been answering any of my calls?" Cruz said in a panic.

"I didn't have my phone," Dylan said flustered.

"It doesn't even matter. All that matters is that you're back." Cruz squeezed her even tighter.

"Is it okay if I come in," Dylan asked, struggling to breathe.

"My bad. Come in." Cruz pulled her inside. "You want something to drink? You hungry?"

"No, I'm good," she insisted. "I just really wanna talk to you."

"Me too," Cruz agreed. "Look, I know that everything between us has happened really quickly."

"Yeah, that's kinda what I wanted to talk to you about?" Dylan sat on the edge of the couch.

"Dig this." Cruz sat down beside her. "I know that we got engaged really fast and that I asked you to marry me in a month—"

"Cruz." Dylan tried to speak again.

"No, let me finish. I was wrong for rushing you. I should've understood that you needed some time. But I want you to know that I'm not mad at you. Everyone gets cold feet—"

"Cruz," Dylan interjected.

"No let me speak," Cruz stressed. "I love you Dylan and if you want to get married today, tomorrow or next year it doesn't matter. I'm willing to wait on you 'cause that's how important to me you are."

"Cruz!" Dylan yelled, praying this time he'd listen. "Oh my god! Will you shut up?"

"My bad." He calmed down. "You're right. Go ahead and speak."

"Whew." She let out a sigh of relief. "Oh my god this is so hard."

"Take your time?" He massaged her arm.

"I wish I knew how to say this." Dylan paused and looked at him. "I really do care about you and my intentions were never to hurt you."

"I know," Cruz nodded.

23

"But … while I was gone I did something." Dylan swallowed hard.

"Did what?"

"Oh my gosh this is hard." Dylan ran her hands down her face.

"Just say it," Cruz said adamantly.

"I got married."

"What?" Cruz looked confused.

"Angel and I got married."

Dylan gazed into Cruz's eyes. She wished she could tell what he was thinking but his face was stone. All she could see was the tears that were building in his eyes. This was the moment she'd dreaded since she and Angel said I do. She didn't want to hurt Cruz. He hadn't deserved the. pain she was causing him but her heart belonged to Angel and it always would.

"Cruz?" She whispered. "Are you okay?"

"Yeah, I'm straight." He stood up and paced the room.

"Understand that it's not you, it's me." Dylan tried her best to explain. "I should've been honest with you from the jump and told you how I really felt. Instead of letting things go this far. I had no business accepting your proposal when I knew I still had feelings for Angel. I am so

24

sorry and I pray that you can forgive me. Can you ever forgive me?"

"Yeah, sure." He nodded his head. "I forgive you." He furiously punched his fist through the wall.

"What the hell?" Dylan jumped.

"FUCK!" Cruz flung his wrist up and down from the pain.

"Are you okay?" Dylan rushed over to inspect his hand.

"Does it look like I'm fuckin' okay?" Cruz reared his hand back and slapped Dylan so hard that she torpedoed across the room.

"You fuckin' crazy!" He stormed over to where she lay on the floor. "I could kill yo' ass right now! How the fuck you gon' come here and tell me some shit like that and think everything gon' be good?"

Dylan turned over onto her side and touched her lip. The trickles of blood on her fingertips revealed that her lip was busted.

"I can't believe you fuckin' hit me?" She sat on her butt and scooted back.

"I fuckin' loved you! How could you do this to me?" Spit spewed from Cruz's mouth. "That nigga played the shit outta you and this is how you do me?"

"I'm sorry," Dylan cried.

"You sorry? Yeah, you's a sorry muthafucka, alright!" Cruz tossed a lamp across the room.

Afraid for her life Dylan got up and tried running towards the door but Cruz grabbed her by the back of her shirt and pulled her towards him.

"Where the fuck you think you going?" He spun her around.

"Get the fuck off of me!" Dylan kneed him in the groan.

Cruz cupped his dick and bent over in agony. Seeing that she had a way out Dylan quickly picked up her purse and raced out of the door.

"Dylan, wait! I'm sorry!" Cruz groaned. "Come back!"

But just like at their wedding there was no way Dylan was turning back. After this Cruz would never see her face again.

For almost two hours, Dylan drove around in circles, dreading going home. She thought things were bad at first but now things were worse. Angel was sure to flip when he saw her face and there was no telling what he might do to her or Cruz after witnessing the damage. Dylan was beyond paranoid and upset. For the first time in years she didn't have a stitch of press powder or foundation in her purse to cover up the red hand print on the side of her face. Thank god she had a pair of Tom Ford sunnies and a Louis Vuitton scarf in her glove compartment to conceal the remnants of Cruz smack down.

Dylan didn't know how she'd hide her busted lip though. Building up all the courage she had, Dylan placed on her shades and draped the scarf around her head and tied it underneath her neck. Taking a much needed breath she unlocked the door and prayed for the best. After climbing the steps leading to her kitchen she spotted Angel standing in front of the refrigerator.

Angel was the epitome of fine. His brash behavior and cocky attitude was a turn on to Dylan. It didn't hurt that he was six feet two and 220 pounds of pure muscle. He rocked a bald and thick beard like no other. His skin reminded her of the sun. On his chest in cursive letter were the words "Death Before Dishonor". The tribal tattoo that reached from the right side of his shoulder all the way down to his ankle made Dylan want to ride his dick every time she laid eyes on him.

"Where you been?" He asked, looking for something to eat.

"Umm, I ran to the mall," Dylan lied.

"You didn't buy the whole mall did you?" Angel finally looked her way.

"No." Dylan gazed off to the side.

"That's an interesting look you got going on," he laughed. "What you call that, the Jackie O?"

"How'd you guess?" Dylan laughed nervously, concealing her face with her hand.

"Why you actin' so weird? What's wrong wit' you?" Angel stood up straight and looked at her.

"Nothin'. I just gotta pee." Dylan tried to walk away.

"Ah uh." Angel blocked her path.

"What?" Dylan put her head down.

"What's wrong wit' you? And take this silly ass scarf off." Angel tried to untie it.

"No!" Dylan yelled, slapping his hand away. "Stop!"

"What the fuck is yo' problem?"

"Nothin'. I told you I gotta use the bathroom." She lied again.

"Let me look at you first." Angel lifted her head.

Fed up with trying to hide the inevitable Dylan allowed him to see her face without struggle. With her scarf and shades off, Angel took one look at her face and said, "Who whooped yo' ass?"

"Nobody. Now can I please go and use the bathroom?"

"Lie to me again," Angel warned.

"I'm not lyin'." Dylan rolled her eyes.

"Did Milania fuck you up?" Angel eyed her quizzically.

"Boy please." Dylan shot furiously. "Don't make me fuck you up."

"Then what happened and tell the truth this time."

Dylan inhaled deeply and sighed.

"Promise me you won't get mad."

"Tell me what happened first." Angel replied, unwilling to fold.

"No. Not until you promise me you won't get mad," Dylan demanded.

"A'ight, I promise," Angel lied. "Now where you been?"

"Okay, after I had lunch with Billie and Tee-Tee I went to the Lumière hotel."

"What you go there for?" Angel folded his arms across his chest.

"To see Cruz." Dylan winced, closing her eyes.

"You did what?" Angel said, outraged.

"You promised you weren't gonna get mad?" Dylan stomped her foot like a child.

"Fuck that! What the fuck you go see him for? What you having second thoughts or something?"

"Really, Angel?" Dylan looked at him as if he were stupid.

"No. I went to see him to tell him that I was sorry for running out like that but when I got there he thought that I was coming back to be with him. So when I told him you and I were back together and married," Dylan began to cry, "he flipped out on me."

"That muthafucka hit you?" Angel balled his fist.

"Yeah, he just … lost it. He started throwing things and grabbing me. It was like I didn't even know who he was," Dylan sobbed.

"You shouldn't have taken yo' ass over there in the first place! You don't owe that muthafucka no explanation!"

"But—"

"But nothin'! If that muthafucka didn't get the hint that it was over when you walked out on his ass then oh the fuck well! You had no business going to see him, Dylan. Especially without tellin' me!"

"So, are you sayin' it's my fault I got hit? All I was tryna' do was the right thing, Angel. What I did to him was wrong and all I was tryna' to do is apologize so excuse me for having a fuckin' conscious!" Dylan spat.

"It's not about that! It's about you lettin' me know what the fuck is going on so shit like this won't happen!"

"Well, excuse me for living!"

"Whateva, I'm up." Angel announced, grabbing his keys.

"Where you going?" Dylan asked, praying he wasn't leaving for good.

"To pick up my son!"

Normally, Angel wouldn't yell at Dylan for doing something he didn't like and then turn around and do the same damn thing but in this case rules were meant to be broken. There was no way on God's green earth that he could allow Cruz to get away with putting his hands on his woman. He was tired of being Mr. Nice Guy. It was time for people to understand why he'd become a boxer. It was time to put an end to all the drama once and for all. At any cost Angel, Dylan, and Mason were going to have a normal, peaceful life, even if his life depended on it. After parking, speaking with the concierge and boarding the elevator, Angel got off on the tenth floor and knocked on Cruz's door.

"I knew you'd come back." Angel could hear Cruz say from the other side of the door.

"Baby, I'm sorry for puttin' my hands on you. I just got upset. I swear it won't happen again." Cruz pulled the door back and came face to face with Angel.

"You damn right it won't happen again." Angel's killer instinct kicked in and he blacked out.

An hour later, Angel returned home with Mason as promised. Dylan was in bed asleep. Despite the bruise on her face there was no denying her beauty. Dylan was 5 feet 6 and possessed the creamiest honey colored skin. Her eyes shined like diamonds. She had the perfect heart shaped mouth. Angel often found his self dying to kiss her lips. Dylan had a body most chicks would die for. She could rock anything straight off the rack. She and Rihanna could've been twins.

"Baby." He nudged her thigh.

"Huh." She turned over and looked at him.

"You still love me?" Angel kissed her on the cheek.

Dylan nodded her head and smiled. She could never stay mad at Angel long. The sight of his handsome face alone made her heart melt.

"You love Mason?" He sat him in front of her.

"Of course." Dylan pulled her son into her arms and kissed him all over his face.

"My bad for going off like that," Angel apologized.

"I'm sorry too. I shouldn't have gone over there without telling you first."

"It's all good man. I ain't even trippin' off that shit no more."

"What took you so long to come back?" Dylan rubbed her eyes.

"I had to take care of some last minute business first." Angel pretended to go through his phone to avoid eye contact.

"Just tell me you didn't do anything that could get you in trouble," Dylan said, as a jolt of panic went through her.

"Look at mommy playin' detective. She need a part on CSI don't she Mason?" Angel tickled the baby's stomach.

"Just answer the question," Dylan demanded.

"Everything's good." Angel assured. "You hungry? I bought home some Chinese food."

"Hell yeah. You know I never pass up a meal and I hope you got me some crab rangoon."

I can not see tomorrow if you're
not in my tomorrow.
-Jhene Aiko, "You vs. Them"

Chapter 3

"I guess married life agrees with her. This heffa finally arrived somewhere on time," Tee-Tee said to Billie as Dylan and Mason entered Benton Park Café for breakfast.

"You better leave my sister in-law alone."

"Oooooh she got on shades," Tee-Tee whispered. "Cruz must've really got in dat ass."

"Shut up." Billie hit the top of his hand.

"I'm just sayin'."

"Hello ladies!" Dylan spoke cheerfully.

"Hey girl," Tee-Tee waved. "How yo' eye feelin'?"

"The same as yo' asshole, trick."

Dylan sat Mason inside a high chair then took off her shades.

"Aww shit, I thought you was puffed up underneath them glasses," Tee-Tee flicked his wrist, disappointed.

"Right. You made it seem like Cruz boom bopped yo' ass." Billie laughed.

"He did. My face was red for a couple of hours. My lip is still healing but I'm good. Nothin' can keep this pretty girl down." Dylan waved her head like she had long hair.

"Ughh whatever." Tee-Tee clicked his tongue as if he had a bad taste in his mouth.

"So what's the tea chicas? Why was it a must that we have breakfast today?" Dylan took a sip of water.

"Since you and my brother ran off and eloped Tee-Tee and I have decided to throw ya'll a lavish reception at the 360 Rooftop Bar next Saturday," Billie beamed.

"For real?" Dylan's face lit up.

"Yes ma'am and it's gonna be fabulous. Kate Middleton and Kim K's wedding reception won't have nothin' on yours boo boo," Tee-Tee snapped his fingers.

"Oooh I'm so excited. Mason, that means I get to buy you another tuxedo." Dylan pinched his cheeks. "Oooh and I can wear my wedding dress again," she clapped.

"I think not," Billie disagreed. "My brother would have a fit."

"Aww yeah, you're right," Dylan poked out her bottom lip. "That would be a fashion faux pas."

"The good part about it is we get to go back to Mrs. Wang and buy another dress. But this time instead of a ball gown I'm gonna go for a mermaid style dress." Dylan danced in her seat.

37

"Loves it," Billie agreed.

"Well, it's settled then," Tee-Tee raised his glass for a toast. "Get ready to party bitches!"

Listening to Kelly Rowland's melodic, heartfelt tune *Keep It Between Us,* Dylan pulled into the parking lot of Angel's gym. With the car in park she closed her eyes and sang at the top of her lungs:

"Not a thing in this world,

I won't give up,

Can't live in this world,

If I'm not next to you."

Dylan was so caught up in the words and her emotions that she forgot that she couldn't sing worth a damn which caused her to scare the shit out of Mason who had began to cry.

"Oh honey, I'm sorry." Dylan turned around in her seat and rubbed his knee.

"Mama didn't mean to scare you. Come on let's go see daddy." She turned off the engine, grabbed her purse and got out.

Walking around to the opposite side of the car she opened the door and unbuckled Mason's car seat. With him

38

securely in her arm, she closed the door, chirped the alarm and sashayed inside the gym. Immediately the sound of Angel's fist hitting the pads engulfed her ears. Dylan loved to watch Angel train. Everything about him was primal and methodical. The killer instinct that he tried his hardest to conceal outside of the ring was on full display. His overpowering strong physique and aggressive intensity sent chills up her spine. She was sure to get a piece of him later on that night.

"Time!" Angel's timekeeper yelled, after he'd beaten the bag to a pulp.

Breathing in and out, Angel paced back and forth until he spotted Dylan and Mason out of the corner of his eye. Even when she wasn't trying to do the most, Dylan always looked impeccable. The other men in the room tried not to ogle at her but no man could take their eyes off of Dylan. She was sexy beyond words.

That afternoon she was casually dressed in a mustard colored, Silence & Noise blouse with the sleeves rolled up, printed booty shorts, a camel colored vintage clutch and 1920's inspired, crystal ankle strap, Jimmy Choo platforms with a plexiglass heel. The shorts highlighted her firm toned legs and round, plump ass.

"How long you been standing there pretty girl?" Angel wiped the sweat off his face with a towel and walked over to her.

"Just for a minute." Dylan smiled, looking him up and down.

His muscles were out of control.

"You lookin' at me like you wanna do something."

"Oh I do," She licked her bottom lip suggestively.

"Not in front of my son," Angel joked, kissing Mason on the cheek. "C'mon man." He took Mason from Dylan's arms.

"Daddy wanna show you some moves. Mommy you come and get in the ring too."

"You gon' show me some moves later on?" Dylan flirted.

"It's going down tonight. You gon' get nasty for me?" Angel held the rope up for her.

"You ain't even gotta ask twice, daddy." Dylan climbed inside the ring. "Now what's up?" She bounced around, throwing jabs at the air.

"What you gon' teach me and Mason?"

"First of all, Apollo Creed, calm down before you break something."

"Whatever," Dylan rolled her eyes. "You know I know how to throw them thangs."

"Uh huh," Angel nodded his head mockingly. "Mason, yo' mama think she a thug."

"I am. Westside fool." Dylan threw up a W with her fingers. "Ooh babe I forgot to tell you Billie and Tee-Tee are gonna throw us a reception next Saturday at the Three Sixty Rooftop Bar."

"That's what's up."

"So, I was thinkin' about buying a new dress," Dylan batted her eyes and turned from side to side like a little kid.

"I don't care Dylan. That's if you already haven't. Knowing yo' ass you probably have already bought like five dresses."

"O ye, of little faith," Dylan grinned because Angel was right.

"Yeah a'ight, I know you did."

"Okay, but you were wrong. I only bought three. They all were so cute I couldn't decide. I swear babe you're gonna love whichever one I pick."

"All I know is this better be the baddest dress I've ever seen."

As promised Dylan's dress not only wowed Angel but all of their family and friends as well. She stunned the crowd in a 60's inspired, pale pink, feathered trimmed; Marchesa, baby doll dress and nude peep toe Christian Louboutin five inch heels. But as much as everyone was in awe of Dylan's outfit she was even more impressed by the venue. The Three Sixty Rooftop Bar was constructed atop the 25-story east tower of the Hilton hotel and offered a 360-degree view indoor and out, of the riverfront, Arch, city skyline and Busch stadium.

And although Dylan's dress was a show stopper, nothing could compare to the outstanding décor of the bar. The sleek, urban space featured a giant outside bar, several indoor bars, dozens of flat-screen TVs, Zen-like fire pits and several private and semi-private dining spaces. On each of the tables were centerpieces made of white roses, and orchids. Once again Billie and Tee-Tee had outdone themselves. Dylan didn't know how on earth she'd be able to repay them for their love and generosity.

"Do you love it?" Billie gleamed walking towards her with open arms.

"I die," Dylan hugged her. "I mean Billie this is like on another level."

42

"I think I need to add party planner to my list of careers, if I do say so myself." Billie dusted off her shoulder.

"Ah uh honey, you don't need no more jobs on yo' resume." Tee-Tee chimed in. "You're already overqualified."

"Bye Fa'Hater!" Billie put her hand in his face.

"Girl bye," Tee-Tee said with a laugh.

"An-y-way you look FIERCE mama!" He snapped his fingers.

"Thanks boo boo," Dylan curtsied. "You look hot too. I'm loving the Basketball Wives Miami look you got going on." Dylan admired the one shoulder, blue sequined dress he wore.

"It's cool. I already know I'm hot." Angel shrugged his shoulders and posed.

The John Varvatos tuxedo he donned fit his body like a glove.

"Baby, you are too fine for words." Tee-Tee winked his eye at him.

"Yo." Angel furrowed his brows and curled his lip.

"Alright, alright," Tee-Tee stomped his foot. "Yo' outfit tight dog." He said in his lower register.

"Eww you sound like a fool," Dylan laughed.

"Why you think I look like this?" He ran his hands down his hips. "Me and butch just don't mix."

"You got that right," Billie agreed.

"CHUNKY!" Candy, Dylan's mother, came stumbling towards her.

As always Candy had a drink in her hand and was dressed like a hooker fresh off the hoe stroll. Dylan thought she was out there with her fashion but her mother took the cake. It was like she pulled the most sluttish outfit she could find. She wore a black, tube dress with cut out slits going down the side of the dress, revealing the fact that she wore no panties and patent leather, platform, over the knee boots.

"Hello mother." Dylan spoke dryly.

"What the hell are you wearing? Why you dressed like Betty White?" Candy tuned up her face.

"Ooh ma." Dylan examined her leg. "You got a run in your stocking. Oh, sorry, it's just a spider vein."

"Touché," Candy raised her glass then took a long drink.

"On the real Candy, you look hot," Angel said, chuckling.

"Don't make a black girl blush," Candy smiled, coyly.

"Speaking of sexy, here come trouble," Tee-Tee shot a devilish grin.

"Ah uh who invited him?" Billie glared at State, Dylan's ex-fiancé.

He'd just gotten off the elevator and was searching the room for someone he knew. For over three years Dylan and State were in an on-again off-again relationship. They were even engaged for a short while but after State announced that he didn't want to be a father or a husband, the two broke up. Unable to let him go, Dylan found herself right back in his arms only to learn that he'd gotten married to someone else. For a while, she didn't speak to him but Dylan and State had an unshakable bond that many couldn't understand. They now were strictly friends, who called upon one another for advice and support.

"I did, now do something." Dylan jumped at her.

"But nobody wants him here." Billie ignored her sarcasm.

"I do," Dylan snapped.

"Why?" Angel mean mugged her. "Don't you think you should've run this by me first?"

"Umm," Dylan said, caught off guard by his attitude. "No, I didn't think it was a big deal. You know State and I are friends."

"Yeah, okay." Angel's nostril's flared as State neared.

"Look at you. You wearing that dress ma." State wrapped his arms around Dylan's waist and squeezed her tight.

"Thank you." Dylan eased back from the hug quickly.

"So you finally got married, huh?"

"Yes, sir. You remember Angel don't you?" Dylan stood beside her man.

"Congratulations, my dude." State held out his hand for a shake.

"I'ma go get me something to drink." Angel ignored him and walked away.

"Somebody got an attitude," Tee-Tee whispered.

"Sorry about that. He'll come around sooner or later." Dylan tried her best to smooth over the uncomfortable situation.

"It's all good. I think I should go though," State replied, feeling unwelcome.

"Good idea." Billie cut him off.

"You're not going anywhere." Dylan gave Billie the evil eye.

"Nah, I'ma burn out. I ain't come to start a bunch of confusion," State insisted.

"I'm tellin' you. It's totally cool." Dylan tried to assure him.

"Umm can I speak to you alone for a minute," Billie asked, Dylan.

"Yeah."

"We'll be right back." Billie smirked pulling Dylan away by the arm.

"What is your problem?" Dylan yanked her arm away.

"Listen let me give you a crash course in marriage 101. You do not and I repeat do not invite your ex fiancé to any function especially not your reception unless you wanna get shot."

"But State and I are just friends. I look at him like a brother now. If it wasn't for him I wouldn't have my book deal or my show."

"So the hell what? How would you feel if Angel invited Milania?"

Suddenly a wave of redness rushed over Dylan.

"You know I hadn't even looked at it that way. You're right. I shouldn't have invited him. But he's here now and I don't wanna tell him to leave."

47

"No problem. I will." Billie marched towards him only to be stopped by the party planner.

"Mrs. Christianson can I speak with you for a moment? We're having a problem with the entertainment for the night."

"Sure," Billie said, hesitantly.

As Billie and the party planner walked to the back of the room, Kyrese, her son made his way over to State. This was the perfect opportunity for him to get the autograph he'd been dying for.

"Hey, you're State, right?" Kyrese asked, curiously.

"Yeah." State looked down at the li'l boy.

"Like the State," Kyrese beamed. "Grammy award winning, State?"

"Yeah li'l man and who are you?"

"Aww, my bad. I'm Kyrese. My old bird is the chick over there in the too little black dress," Kyrese pointed.

"Billie's your mother?" State questioned shocked.

"Yeah, but that's nothin', back to you. Like on the real you're my idol," Kyrese stressed, excited. "When I grow up I wanna be just like you. Even though my mom says being a record producer ain't no real job."

"Oh word? That's what she said," State sucked his teeth.

"Yeah but I don't pay her no mind. Ay, can I have yo' autograph? Every time I ask my mom to get one from you she always says no." Kyrese handed State a napkin.

"That sounds like Billie alright." State wrote his name.

"Yo I can't wait to show everybody in my class this. The honeys really gon' be on me now. You know everybody at my school say I look just like you."

"You don't look nothin' like him," Kenzie, Kyrese's sister came from nowhere and butted in.

"Right," Kaylee, Kenzie's twin sister agreed. "You ugly. He fine."

"Shut up!" Kyrese barked.

As the kids argued, for the first time since Kyrese approached him, State took a good look at the boy. The kids at his school were right. He did look like him, too much like him. They both had skin the color of midnight and smoldering brown eyes. Like Kyrese when he was a young boy, State too was slightly chubby. But what stood out the most was the mole under Kyrese's right eye. It was the same exact mole that was under States eyes.

"Why don't you gone somewhere and get you some business lil' stupid dumb girl!" Kyrese snapped.

"Make me!" Kaylee crossed her arm across her chest.

"I'ma beat yo' butt if ya'll don't get some where and sit down," Billie interjected, breaking up the argument. "Kyrese you know better."

"What? I didn't even do nothin'," Kyrese said with an attitude.

"Yeah, yeah, yeah go sit down wit' Knox. I'll be over there in a second."

"Huuuuuuh, I never get to do nothin' fun. I'ma holla at you State." Kyrese said, sadly walking away.

"A'ight man," State said bye.

"Look-a-here," Billie got up in State's face. "For some odd reason Dylan wants you here. I, of course don't, so please do us both a favor and stay the hell away from me and my kids."

"That's cool but I got one question for you." State responded not backing down.

"What?" Billie cocked her head to the side.

"Is he mine?"

"Is who yours?" Billie tried to pretend like her heart wasn't beating out of her chest.

"Your son, Kyrese. Is he mine?" State gazed deep into her eyes.

Billie swallowed hard. Since the day she learned she was pregnant with Kyrese she'd done everything in her power to avoid this moment. But being the control freak she was, just in case she was ever hit with unwanted questioning she'd practiced what she would say. But now that the moment was here Billie felt trapped. It felt like with every breathe she took the entire world was closing in on her.

"No, he's not. His father is Cain Townsend. Now, if you don't mind I have a party to tend to so please once again leave."

"You know if I find out different me and you gon' have problems," State said firmly.

"Why are you still talkin'? You should be in your car heading home by now," Billie shot back unfazed by his threat.

"Tell Dylan I'll holla at her later." State eyed Billie skeptically before leaving.

With her head held high and her shoulders back, Billie watched as State boarded the elevator. Once the elevator doors closed and he was out of sight, she let out a huge sigh of relief. She'd come too far for State to go poking his nose in her life now. No matter the cost she had to keep her secret buried because if the truth was ever revealed she'd lose everything important in her life.

Across the room Dylan searched the crowd for her husband. She was determined to make things right between them. Spotting him by the bar Dylan sauntered over to where he was. Standing behind him, she wrapped her arms around his waist and whispered, "I'm sorry."

"You sure are." Angel took a swig of his drink.

"Heeeeeey," Dylan playfully hit him on the arm.

"You know I'm just fuckin' wit' you." Angel turned and faced her.

"You better be," Dylan laughed. "For real I apologize for not asking you would it be okay to invite State. I should've been more considerate of your feelings."

"Yeah you should've but it's all good, shorty. Tonight we're celebrating. I ain't tryin' to beef wit' you. Just keep him away from me."

"Eye-eye captain." Dylan saluted him.

"Excuse me, Mr. Carter?" A male voice interrupted their conversation.

"Yes." Angel turned around.

"You're under arrest. Anything you say can and will be held against you." The officer said as he handcuffed him.

"What the hell is going on?" Dylan shrieked. "My husband hasn't done anything. Let go of him." She tried to push the officer away.

"Ma'am if you touch him again we're going to place you under arrest too." The other officer warned.

"Fuck that! This is my husband!"

"Dylan chill!" Angel tried to calm her down.

"Dylan, what's going on?" Billie rushed over.

"I don't know. They're arresting him," Dylan cried.

"Excuse me. I'm Billie, Angel's sister. Can you please let us know what is happening?"

"We are placing Mr. Carter under arrest for assault," the officer replied.

"Assaulting who?"

"A mister," The officer looked down at his pad. "Javier Cruz."

"What?" Dylan looked at Angel. "Angel, you didn't."

"Just call my lawyer!" Angel said as he was escorted out of the room.

"Okay." Dylan sniffled shaking her head.

"Everything gon' be cool." Angel promised as he watched tears fall from Dylan's eyes.

Usually Dylan believed her husband when he made promises. Something deep within her soul was telling her that this was just the beginning of her and Angel's problems, and no matter how much she prayed there was no stopping.

What's going on in that beautiful mind?
-John Legend, "All of Me"

Chapter 4

Ten hours later after being booked and processed Dylan was able to post Angel's bail and take him home where he rightfully belonged. But before he could take a shower, grab something to eat and hit the sheets Angel had some major explaining to do.

"So are you ready to tell me what happened, jail bird?" Dylan folded her arms across her chest and leaned against the frame of the bathroom door.

"Seriously, Dylan?" Angel looked at her sideways as he unbuttoned his shirt revealing his firm pecks and rock hard abs.

Although Dylan was majorly pissed at him the visual of his taut physique caused her to temporarily lose her breath but Dylan couldn't allow her attraction to her husband to take over. She had to stay focused.

"Don't seriously Dylan me. I asked you fifty million times if there was something you needed to tell me and you said no, Bone Thugs and Harmony."

"Ha-ha funny." Angel took off his pants and threw them into the dirty clothes hamper. "Enough of the jail jokes."

"Mmm," Dylan popped her lips. "Excuse me. Let me shut my mouth then before I get shanked. I ain't about that prison life, ya' feel me."

"You can stop now," Angel warned.

"Then tell me the truth. What happened?"

"I didn't tell you cause I didn't want you to get upset but the night you came home after gettin' into it wit' ole boy I went to go see him."

"Please don't tell me you went and put them paws on him, Scrappy."

"Yeah, I did ignorant ass," Angel couldn't help but laugh.

"But why babe? I handled it."

"You ain't handle shit. He slapped the shit outta you. He needed his ass whooped," Angel turned on the shower.

"But you know you can't go around putting your hands on people. Your hands are considered lethal weapons," Dylan shot sternly.

"I know but you're my wife. I couldn't let that shit ride."

"Now you have an assault case. What if you have to go to jail?" Tears formed in Dylan's eyes. "I'm not writing yo' ass no letters and I'm most certainly not accepting no high ass collect calls."

"That's not gon' happen."

"You don't know that." Dylan's bottom lip trembled.

"And neither do you cry baby so stop crying." Angel wiped her tears away.

"I couldn't take it if that happened."

"It's not." He held her close. "I'm not gon' let nothin' bad happen."

"I hope not." Dylan closed her eyes and listened to the soothing sound of his heartbeat. "I hope not."

"GIVE ME BACK MY SON!" Billie screamed, jumping out of her sleep in a cold sweat.

"Baby, are you okay?" Knox asked, rubbing her arm.

Billie wanted to answer him but she couldn't catch her breath. All she could focus on was the darkness surrounding her and the rapid thump of her heart.

"Billie," Knox shook her. "Baby, answer me. Are you okay?"

Billed looked at his face and took a deep gulp of air.

"Babe you're shaking like a leaf." Knox brushed her hair out of her face.

Billie didn't even recognize that she was shaking so bad. The terrifying dream she had shook her to the core of her soul. She was so terrified that she couldn't decipher if her being awake was a dream or reality.

"Billie do you hear me?" Knox shook her again. "Are you alright?"

"Huh?" She stared at him with a vacant look in her eye.

"You had a nightmare baby." Knox caressed her face. "Look at you. You're all sweaty. What were you dreaming about?"

"I-I-I don't remember." Billie lied quickly.

"You woke up screaming give me back my son."

"I did?" Billie swallowed hard.

"Yeah, did you have a dream about Kyrese?" Knox asked, worried.

"My throat is really dry. Let me go get a drink of water," Billie eased out of bed; avoiding the question.

Inside the master bathroom Billie closed and locked the door to ensure her privacy. With the light on Billie gazed at her reflection in the mirror. She was a wreck. Her hair was disheveled and she was shaking like a drug addict. She hated what she saw staring back at her. What she saw staring back at her was the scared twenty-three year old girl with the weight of the world on her shoulders.

She despised that girl. That girl was a stupid, naive, fool. She was out of control, reckless and hopelessly in love with a man she knew would break her heart. A man that took control of her heart then cast it away like it was trash. For years Billie buried that vulnerable, tarnished girl deep inside her subconscious and vowed never to revisit her again.

But here she was live in the flesh with tears the size of lemon drops in her eyes. All of her mistakes, lies, and secrets were bubbling onto the surface. She had to put the lid on them and keep them hidden. No one could know the real Billie because if they did they wouldn't like her. Hell, sometimes she didn't even like herself. If her family and friends knew the real her they would surely abandon her and in all actuality, she couldn't blame them if they did.

Sick with worry Billie swiftly splashed cold water onto her face and tried her damnest to erase the horrible dream she had. After drying her face with a warm towel she turned off the light and went back to bed. Knox was up waiting for her return.

"Are you alright? You scared the shit outta me."

"Yeah," Billie released a small laugh. "It was just a silly dream."

"You sure 'cause you seemed pretty shaken up about it?" Knox kept fishing for answers.

"Baby," Billie pulled the covers up to her chest. "I'm fine. I just had a nightmare. It's no big deal. You can go back to sleep now." She gave him a quick peck on the cheek.

"A'ight." Knox eyed her quizzically before turning off the bedside light.

Knox still felt the need to comfort his wife so he slid over to her side of the bed and wrapped her up in his arms. Calmed by his touch, Billie inhaled deep and exhaled out her worries but as soon as Knox drifted off to sleep the still of the night consumed her. It suffocated her lungs. No matter how hard she tried to ease the alarming thoughts that plagued her mind, they kept resurfacing; reminding her that darkness didn't just come at night. For Billie, darkness was looming ahead.

Like Lady Gaga, Dylan lived for the applause. Being famous gave her a sense of purpose. She loved the notoriety and acclaim. But sometimes being a part of Hollywood's elite wasn't all it was cracked up to be. Since Angels' arrest the paparazzi stalked their every move. Dylan couldn't leave the confines of her home without camera lenses being shoved down her throat. Usually she lived for the free publicity but now the shit was just plain annoying.

Once the media got wind of Angel assaulting Cruz and the back story behind it, a media firestorm brewed. Dylan, Angel and Cruz crazy love triangle was splashed across every major tabloid magazine, blog and entertainment news show. Now that Angel was officially being charged with assault and could face up to five years in prison, the paparazzi went into over drive trying to get statements and pictures.

Dylan longed for the days she could go around semi unnoticed. She longed to be able to spend quality time with her family and friends without some random photographer invading her privacy. On that particular day she and Billie were at the BCBG MAX AZRIA store in Frontenac Plaza having a private viewing of all their latest merchandise.

One of the great perks of being a celebrity or socialite was being able to shut down an entire store and shop without the interruption of people asking for pictures and autographs.

Plus Dylan always got first dibs on the hottest and latest clothes and shoes before anyone else. Dressed head to toe in denim, Dylan rocked a denim button up shirt, unbuttoned to the center of her chest with no bra. A pearl Chanel pin rested on the breast pocket of the top. The rest of the look consisted of a ripped denim skirt, Chanel lucite cuff bracelet and nude Louboutin Pigalle heels. In love with BCBG's fall collection, Dylan sipped on a chilled glass of rosé champagne while sifting through racks of beautiful dresses. She was so consumed in the clothing that she hadn't even noticed that Billie wasn't as into it and was casually scrolling through the store aimlessly.

"This is sick." Dylan held up a $400 black and white evening dress with a thigh high slit. "Ooh and this leather pullover is sick," she gushed.

"I can't get with that look. That's a lil' too hood for me." Billie looked at the top as if it stunk. "I haven't worn a pullover since college."

"You ain't about that life," Dylan laughed.

"I sholl in the fuck ain't," Billie laughed too. "So how is my brother holding up?"

Dylan stopped and sighed.

"As well as can be, I guess. He really doesn't talk about it that much. I guess he's trying to keep a strong face so I won't get scared but it's not working. I'm scared shitless. I mean we've only been married a minute and he already might be taken away from me again. It's like we can't catch a break."

"I know the feeling," Billie mumbled.

"I just wish this whole thing would just go away," Dylan remarked.

"Everything is gonna work out. He's not going to jail," Billie answered, hoping she sounded convincing.

"I hope so. So how have you been? We haven't really been able to talk since the party. By the way, thank you again."

"No problem, we're family girl. But I've just been busy with the kids, Knox and the art museum. I'm drained," Billie confessed.

"You seem stressed out. I can look at you and tell. You sure that's all it is," Dylan asked innocently.

"Yeah," Billie replied, alarmed. "Why would you think it was anything else?"

"I don't know… you just seem… different. I can't really pin point what it is, it's just something."

"I mean I'm nervous about Angel of course. Other than that I don't know what you're picking up on. I'm fine, I swear," Billie persisted.

"Okay calm down. I believe you," Dylan chuckled thrown off by her persistence.

"But you know what? Now that I think about it, you're not the only one who has been actin' strange since the party. State has been acting hella strange too," Dylan thought out loud. "I don't know what happened. After we spoke that negro just up and left without saying goodbye."

"Mmm," Billie turned her back to Dylan so she wouldn't see the look of panic in her eyes.

"Ya'll didn't get into did you? 'Cause I saw ya'll talking for a minute and ya'll know how ya'll do when you're in the same space," Dylan inquired.

"No, not all. Kyrese just wanted an autograph," Billie responded coolly.

"Hmm," Dylan twisted her lips to the side, stumped. "Idk," she shrugged.

"Maybe he had an emergency." Billie tried to throw Dylan off.

"I'ma text him and ask." Dylan pulled out her iPhone 5.

"No!" Billie shrieked, scaring the living daylight out of Dylan.

"What the hell is wrong wit' you?" Dylan stepped back.

"Girl, leave that man alone." Billie came towards her.

"I'm sure he is okay. You ain't heard about him on the 5 o'clock news so he a'ight. Besides we're having a girl's day. State's trifling ass can wait." Billie took Dylan's phone from her hand and slipped it back inside her purse.

"I feel you but," Dylan took the phone back out "that's my homeboy and we look out for each other." She began to text State.

"Well you handle that." Billie grabbed her purse. "I forgot I had a meeting today at 2 o'clock so I gotta jet. Love you to pieces. I'll call you later," Billie air kissed both of Dylan's cheeks and left before she could get a word in edge wise.

I'ma teach you how to love me.
-Chris Brown, "Give it Away"

Chapter 5

The one thing that Dylan cherished the most about being a married woman was coming home every day to her fine ass husband and her adorable, sweet son. She couldn't love anything or anyone more than them. Nothing else compared to their love. Angel was her whole entire world. He meant everything to her. Waking up to his face every morning was like Christmas and New Year's Eve wrapped up in one beautiful ass package.

She simply adored him and vowed to give him her all. From the second Dylan said 'I do' she made a promise to herself, Angel and God that their family would always come first. They would never be apart from each other for more than a few days; go on dates at least once a week and have dinner together as a family every night. Every day after taping her show Edible Couture for the Food Network, Dylan came home and prepared dinner.

It didn't matter how hard her day was or how stressed out she was, cooking dinner for Angel and Mason was a must. It was also somewhat therapeutic. While she cooked it allowed her time to think and reflect on the day.

She and Angel would also share a bottle of wine, vibe out to some music and talk. For dinner that night they were having spaghetti and fried catfish which was a staple in the black community.

Dylan and Angel got a kick out of seeing Mason slurp his chopped up spaghetti noodles.
The homemade tomato sauce Dylan made was all over his mouth and hands but she didn't care. It was dinner time and he could make as big of a mess as he pleased. The maid would be in the next morning to clean anyway. Dylan loved her home, the dining room especially. They had a beautiful, distressed wooden table with stained wooden chairs flown in from Africa.

A colorful bouquet of hydrangea's sat in the center of the table. Miss matched plates and cups from all over the world and silk napkins from India decorated the table. While John Legend's latest album *Love In The Future* played melodically in the background Dylan and Angel enjoyed their meal and discussed the day's events.

"I couldn't make a move today without the paparazzi being all up my ass," Dylan announced, chewing her food.

"Me either but it is what it is. I fucked up and now I gotta pay the consequences." Angel took a bite of fish.

"But you were just trying to defend me, babe," Dylan reasoned. "The media is making it seem like you're some out of control maniac. They're even saying you might be taking steroids and that that's how you've been winning all of your fights."

"We know it's some bullshit so don't even trip."

"But it's tarnishing your reputation, Angel. If you let me make a statement everything will get cleaned up," Dylan stressed.

"Everything will get cleaned up in court." Angel took a sip of wine.

Dylan sat quietly for a while when a thought popped up in her mind.

"What if I talked to Cruz?"

"You out yo' fuckin' mind?" Angel grimaced. "You ain't going no where near that dude."

"I'm talking about over the phone." Dylan tried to explain.

"No, absolutely not. Fuck that nigga. He wanna act like a bitch and press charges then let him. All I was doing was sticking up for my wife."

"Yeah but sticking up for me might land you in jail for five years," Dylan replied, somberly. "We just got back together. I couldn't fathom losing you again."

"You're not," Angel stroked her cheek. "I ain't going no where. I'm right here."

"For now," Dylan rebutted.

"Forever." Angel leaned across the table and kissed her gently on the lips.

It was funny to Dylan how one single kiss from Angel's lips could put all of her worries to rest.

"Have I told you that I love you today," she smiled.

"Nope," Angel shook his head with a grin on his face. "You ain't shit."

"Lies you tell!" Dylan yelled, holding her chest.

"You know I'm just fuckin' wit' you," Angel cracked up laughing.

"Well, I love you-I love you-I love you-I love you," Dylan playfully placed kisses all over his face.

"Stop," Angel scrunched up his face, trying to push her away.

"Oh hush you know you love my kisses," Dylan pushed his arm as her phone started to ring.

"Oooh let me get this, it's State. I sent him a text earlier." She left the room and went into the kitchen unaware that Angel was fuming. "What up fool?"

"You stupid," State chuckled. "What's up?"

"You. Why did you leave the party without saying goodbye?"

"My bad, some shit came up that I wasn't expecting. I meant to tell you I was leaving but I just got caught up."

"Oh okay, let me find out you're hiding something from me," Dylan joked.

"Nah," State replied, nervously. "Never that. What you up to though?" He asked, changing the subject.

"Eating dinner wit' my honey. You hungry? You want a plate?"

"I'm straight. Go ahead and finish eating. I'll hit you up tomor," State spoke.

"A'ight, then lil' big head boy. Bye." Dylan ended the call and returned to the table.

As soon as she sat down, she could tell by the look on Angel's face that he was upset.

"What?" Dylan cocked her head to the side already annoyed.

"You already know what it is so don't even ask." Angel wiped his hands on a napkin.

"You mad because I took a call from State?" Dylan asked, dumbfounded.

"You damn right!" Angel looked at her like she was stupid. "How dare you get up from the table wit' me to go talk to that nigga. And you text him earlier? What the fuck you doing texting him? What you fuckin' him, again?" Angel flipped out.

"No!" Dylan screwed up her face.

"I don't know why you doing your face like that?" Angel shot. "Do I have to remind you that you fucked that nigga while me and you were together? You had a whole side relationship with this dude."

"I know but that's in the past." Dylan waved him off. "Like, I don't even look at him like that no more. He's like a brother to me. We're just friends. When me and you broke up, State and I got tight. He was there for me. Hell, he got me the meeting with Brenda. Without that I would've never got my book deal or my show so I'm not going to be like fuck you."

"Oh word?" Angel mean mugged her. "Okay." He nodded his head.

"Like yo' am I in the fuckin' Twilight zone or something? How do you think that makes me feel to hear that man was there for you while me and you weren't together? So what if I go to jail, he gon' be there for you?"

"Noooooo," Dylan groaned. "I'm telling you that nothing is going on. Why would I even bring him around you if it were?"

"Dylan stop actin' stupid. You know like I know that don't mean shit."

"Oh so now I'm stupid?" Dylan said, stunned.

"The fact that you're sitting here trying to justify this shit is really making me look at you sideways. How would you feel if I was still friends with Milania?" Angel questioned.

"That's different. That bitch is crazy," Dylan countered.

"Get the fuck outta here." Angel scooted his chair back. "You know damn well you wouldn't like it. You feel some type of way when I say hi to a bitch. C'mon man, be real. What you're doing is foul."

"I really don't see it that way. We are just friends. Nothing more, nothing less." Dylan folded her arms across her chest.

"So despite how I feel and everything I got going on you still gon' talk to this man?" Angel asked, one last time.

Instead of answering, Dylan exhaled and rolled her eyes.

"What do you want me to do? He's my friend, that's it." She finally responded.

"You know what?" Angel stood up pissed. "I don't want you to do shit. Go marry that nigga." He threw his napkin down on the table.

Shocked that Angel would hit her with something so cruel and then leave the room Dylan sat silently and looked over at Mason who was staring back at her. Mason had a look on his face as to say mama you done fucked up now.

Hours later after putting Mason to sleep, Angel still wasn't speaking to Dylan. He couldn't understand how she didn't realize that the mere sound of State's name made him enraged. Dylan was the love of his life and to know that she cared for another man as much as she did for him never sat well with him. State was the only other man that Dylan fell head-over-heels in love with.

It took her years to get him out of her system or had she? The fact that she maintained a so called "friendship" with State made Angel wonder was she truly over him? Did a part of her still love him and hold out hope that they could reconcile? Why else would she keep in constant contact with him? She'd hurt Angel in the worst possible way when she'd cheated on him with State.

Angel opened up his heart in ways he'd never had with any other woman only for Dylan to shit on him and fuck another man behind his back. That scar had never fully healed and it never would with State being in the picture. If Dylan didn't recognize that her actions were hurting Angel to the core then that was on her. He had no time to try to make her see otherwise.

Angel was facing up to five years in jail and had a fight to defend his title as heavyweight champion of the world. If Dylan wanted to act like a selfish brat then so be it but he didn't have to tolerate her inconsiderate behavior. If she wanted to remain friends with State, Angel would do what he knew she hated the most, freeze her out. He'd give her his whole ass to kiss as well as the cold shoulder. While preparing for bed they both stood in the bathroom in front of their perspective his and her sinks and brushed their teeth.

Dylan gazed in the mirror at Angel who wouldn't even acknowledge her presence. Normally he'd wink his eye at her or make a funny face while they brushed their teeth but not that night. Angel acted as if Dylan didn't even exist. Dylan knew that he was ignoring her on purpose so she tried not to let it affect her but she failed miserably. She absolutely hated when Angel ignored her. It drove her insane.

An underlining fear that he might leave her again always crept onto the surface causing her anxiety. Dylan wasn't in the business of divorce so she had to make the situation better before it got even worse. Once they were finished brushing their teeth Angel and Dylan climbed into bed. Usually they'd lie in bed and watch television with one another but not that night.

Angel got into bed, turned off the light and closed his eyes without saying a word. Flabbergasted by his childish behavior, Dylan sat up staring into the darkness wondering should she go off or try to have a reasonable conversation with him. Deciding to go the reasonable route; Dylan turned back on the light, pulled Angel over onto his back and straddled him.

"What is it, Dylan? I'm trying to go to sleep," Angel asked, dryly not even looking her in the eye.

"So you just gon' go to sleep and not say goodnight? When we start doing that?"

"Goodnight. Now can you get off of me?" He shot sarcastically.

"No, I can not. Look, I understand where you're coming from but I need you to understand this, I love you and only you. No other man on this earth can compare to you. I don't want anybody else but you. I know what happened between me and State in the past was fucked up but that's exactly what it is, the past. I don't want him and he for damn sure doesn't want me. That ship has sailed and sank like the Titanic. We're just friends and that's all it is and is ever gonna be. I love you and I would never to do anything ever to hurt you. You're my best friend," Dylan said, sincerely.

"I don't wanna fight with you." She leaned down and kissed his lips. "I wanna make love to you." Dylan slid her hand down his stomach and rested her hand on his dick.

Never one to pass up the opportunity to fuck, Angel swiftly tossed Dylan over onto her back. Before she knew it her legs were on his shoulders and he was hitting her with the death stroke. Angel's dick felt like ten inches of pure, adulterated, sin. She could feel it all the way up in her ribcage. A hour later after fuckin' her in every position imaginable Angel and Dylan climaxed.

Dazed from her orgasmic high Dylan lay on her side trying her damnest to catch her breath. She assumed she and Angel would cuddle like they normally do after sex

but Angel had other plans. Just as before, he turned over
and closed his eyes and pretended like she didn't exist.
Dylan's ass was on punishment until further notice. It was
time he teach her a lesson.

If I could forget him, I would.
-Jazmine Sullivan, "I'm in Love
With Another Man"

Chapter 6

A few days later Dylan, Tee-Tee and Billie decided to meet up for lunch at a hip, new Mexican restaurant located in the Central West End called Gringo. Gringo was owned by red blooded American's serving authentic Mexican food with a twist. The restaurant was spacious with wood floors, brightly colored turquoise chairs and chalkboard walls. Dylan welcomed the friendly invite to have lunch with her friends, especially after days of tip toeing around Angel because he was still mad.

Dylan tried waving the white flag numerous times but Angel still wanted to be at war. He was not willing to retreat. It didn't help that Dylan hadn't changed her stance on the subject either. She and State were just friends. She shouldn't have to prove that to Angel. He should automatically trust her and move on. But since that wasn't the case, Dylan decided to pick Billie and Tee-Tee's brain on the subject.

"Yes, you are wrong as hell," Tee-Tee declared. "You're more wrong than Mama's Dee leave out, honey. You're more wrong that Lebron James deformed ass feet."

"Well, goddamn," Dylan giggled. "But nothing is going on between us, that's the thing."

"It might not be but there was something between you two before. Put yourself in his shoes, selfish ass." Tee-Tee retrieved his straw.

"I guess," Dylan responded, not fully convinced.

"Ain't no guess to it, bitch. I'm always right," Tee-Tee joked.

"I frankly don't understand why you want to keep such a vile, disgusting person around you in the first place." Billie chimed in.

She sat all the way back in her seat with her legs crossed and an annoyed expression on her face.

"We've all known from day one State wasn't shit. He treated you and everyone," she stressed, pointing around the table "else in his life like crap."

"Lies you tell. He loves me," Tee-Tee popped his lips.

"He doesn't care about anyone but his self," Billie continued, rolling her eyes. "He will *neveeeer* change. People like him with no heart or conscious are incapable of change."

"Well tell us how you really feel." Dylan's eyes bulged.

"I'm just sayin." Billie sat up straight. "People like him are put on this earth to destroy everyone around them without a thought or care. You really think State care about you? 'Cause if you do you are sadly mistaken. He will chew you up and spit you out honey. He ain't worried about you or your marriage. Hell, he wasn't even worried about his own damn marriage for that matter. He's already made you look crazy enough. Don't end up lookin' like no fool. State is not someone worth having in your life on any term. Trust me, I know."

"What you mean trust me, I know?" Dylan eyed her quizzically.

Realizing she'd said too much, Billie cleared her throat.

"Nothing, I'm just saying I know when a person is being used, that's all," she said, flushing in distress.

"Mmm," Dylan said, not fully convinced.

"You know what I am such an idiot." Billie slapped her hand against her forehead. "Today is my day to pick up the kids from school. Forgive me but I gotta go." She air kissed Dylan and Tee-Tee's cheeks.

"But we haven't even got our food," Tee-Tee objected.

"Don't worry about it. Lunch is on me." Billie yelled over her shoulder leaving out.

"What the hell was that about?" Tee-Tee wondered out loud.

"I have no freaking idea. Homegirl has been on ten since the party. I thought it was just me that noticed it," Dylan said, still taken aback.

"No sweetie, mama is having a full blown nervous breakdown right in front of our eyes. You think its Knox or Cain?" Tee-Tee asked.

"I don't know. She hasn't said anything to me. You know the bitch is weird."

"You's a shady bitch," Tee-Tee cracked up laughing. "Well since lunch is on Billie I think I'm gonna have another margarita. Oh waiter!"

I don't wanna lose you now. I'm lookin' right at the other half of me.
-Justin Timberlake, "Mirror"

Chapter 7

Filming for HBO's 24/7 featuring Angel Carter and Trevor Thomas had begun and the city of St. Louis was on fire. With sports media crews and paparazzi in town all eyes were on the king and queen of the Lou. Angel was pumped and ready for the full on media blitz, non stop training and sparring sessions. His body was in its physical peak and his mind was 100% focused on the bout. Nothing, not even Dylan and her thoughtless bullshit could get him off track.

Since 24/7 was a reality series based on the life of a boxer as he prepares for a fight Angel had to pretend like nothing in his life was off kilter; especially not his marriage to Dylan. They couldn't withstand anymore negative press so when she and Mason arrived to be with him as he trained in front off the press, Angel put on a strong face. He greeted his wife with a sweet kiss. Dylan was overjoyed by the show of affection from her husband.

The heart wrenching silent treatment that he'd been giving her was tearing her apart. She absolutely hated being in the midst of Angel's wrath when he was mad. The man could hold a grudge like no other. She just wished that he could see things her way. She would never betray Angel's trust as she'd done in the past.

If he would only listen to her things between them would be good. By the kiss and the warm hug he gave it seemed like he'd come around. Maybe he finally realized that State was of no threat to him.

"Dylan?" A reporter from ESPN shouted.

"Yes," she smiled, as Angel stood firmly by her side, drinking a bottle of water.

"How have you been keeping up knowing that your husband might be facing five years in jail? Are you afraid?"

"No, I'm not," Dylan said, confidently although she was lying. "My husband did nothing wrong but try to protect me. Once we have our day in court the truth will be revealed."

"My wife is a soldier, that's why I married her." Angel told the reporter.

"Throughout this entire fiasco she's stood by my side and loved me unconditionally. I couldn't ask for a better wife or mother of my son." Angel lovingly kissed Dylan on the forehead causing her heart to flutter.

"Now enough of me sounding like a girl let's get back to boxing." Angel threw on his wickedly addictive charm.

Hours later after hitting the bag, jumping rope and numerous others exercises the media crews left. Angel sat catching his breath while Dylan wiped mounds of sweat from his face.

"You did so good, baby," she gushed, proudly.

"Thanks," Angel replied, dryly. "Come here man." He called out to Mason who was walking around the room.

"Daddy!" Mason wobbled over to his father.

"His little self is getting so big. I wish he could stay this size forever." Dylan poked out her bottom lip.

"Nothing stays the same for too long. You proved that, right?" Angel said, in a brash tone.

"What is that suppose to mean?" Dylan snapped, taken aback by his attitude.

"It means ain't shit changed," Angel stood up with Mason securely in his arms. "You still rock wit' ole boy, right?"

Dylan stood speechless.

"A'ight then," Angel walked away.

Out done by the fact that he was only being nice to her for the cameras, Dylan shook her head. She was tired of the back and forth arguing between her and Angel. This whole thing had to be resolved and fast.

After Angel served his entire firm, ass to Dylan on a platter she left the gym in search of answers. She was still very much conflicted by her views on maintaining a friendship with State. Deciding it was best to go straight to the source, Dylan headed over to State's office building for a chat. Being the media mogul that he was State's office was located in the heart of downtown St. Louis. He had an entire ten floor building that housed his record label, clothing line and staff. As soon as Dylan walked into the building she was greeted by the front desk manager, Laila.

"Dylan. What a surprise," she smiled.

"Hi, I know. I haven't been here in years. I see you all have done some renovations. It looks beautiful." Dylan glanced around at the pristine, white, interior.

"You know Mr. Adanu, everything has to be current and on point."

"Do you and Mr. Adanu have an appointment? "Cause I would've remembered seeing your name on the books." Laila thumbed through the appointment book.

"No, it's a surprise visit. Is he in a meeting because I can talk to him later?" Dylan asked.

"Actually, no. Let me tell him you're coming up." Laila picked up the phone. "Mr. Adanu, Dylan's here to see you."

"Oh word? Send her up," he said.

"Thank you," Dylan mouthed to Laila before boarding the elevator to the tenth floor.

Once she reached her floor, Dylan strutted off the elevator and down the hall to State's office which over looked the city.

"What you doing here Miss?" State greeted her with a hug.

Dylan couldn't deny it, State was the shit. Everything about him was swagged out. His skin was the creamiest shade of dark chocolate. He stood six feet tall and was 200 pounds of pure muscle. His thick English accent made every woman on the planet swoon and the man could rock a suit like no other.

"I need some advice, friend," Dylan groaned, hugging him back.

"Come in and have a seat," State stepped to the side so she could walk into his office.

State's office was massive. The feel was a mix between modernism and tribal chic. Skylights shown brightly from the ceiling. On one side of the room hanging from the wall was a Basquiat painting and mirrors. Underneath the artwork was a white tufted couch with tribal inspired throw pillows. A beautiful marble coffee table with a cheetah print rug sat in front of the couch. Two wooden barrel like chairs and other exquisite pieces such as a glass desk made up the room.

"Can I get you all something to drink or eat?" State's receptionist Essence asked.

"I'm good," Dylan replied, noticing how gorgeous she was.

"Actually, I'll have lunch now," State responded.

"Ok." Essence said before, closing the door behind her.

"You keep a bad bitch around you, don't you," Dylan joked.

"When you're around beautiful things you work hard to maintain it."

"I feel you on that playboy," Dylan laughed, sitting down.

"So what's the deal? What you need my advice on?" State sat across from her.

"My husband," Dylan sighed.

"I don't know nothing about that man," State chuckled. "He don't even like me."

"That's precisely the problem. Angel feels some type of way because you and I are friends. I keep on telling him that it ain't even nothing' like that between me and you no more. I look at you like a brother now."

"Girl … you know you want this dick," State joked, cracking up laughing.

"Really?" Dylan bugged up laughing too.

"I'm just playing but nah I understand where that man is coming from. Me and you had a whole relationship for damn near three years and you smashed me behind his back. Hell, I wouldn't want you to be friends wit' me either."

"Right." Dylan said after a pause.

"I mean that's your husband. I or nobody else should come before that," State continued.

"You're right," Dylan agreed. "When did you become so damn wise?"

"The moment I lost you."

"Aww poor baby. You'll be a'ight." She tickled his side.

"So what's been up wit' your homegirl?" State questioned, as Essence brought in his lunch.

"Who?"

"Billie." State opened up his sandwich and soup.

"Why are you asking me about Billie? You can't stand her." Dylan asked, caught off guard by the question.

"I don't know," State shrugged. "She just popped up in my mind for some reason."

"She's cool, I guess. I think it's something going on with her but she just ain't telling me."

"What you think it is?" State quizzed, fishing for answers.

"I don't know, maybe she's having marital problems. I don't know. She just seems on edge lately."

"Mmm." State nodded his head, chewing his food. "Hopefully she'll be a'ight."

"Yeah, hopefully but anyway I'm gettin' ready to go home and twerk for my husband."

"Wit' what, your back? 'Cause you sholl ain't got no ass," State teased.

"Fuck you," Dylan laughed, throwing a napkin at his head.

Don't let this shit come between
us. I'm wrong, you're right.
-Chris Brown, "I Can't Win"

Chapter 8

After another full workout at the gym, Angel returned home that night exhausted. All he wanted was a hot meal and a bed. He didn't have time for any long drawn out conversations with Dylan about feelings. Angel was simply not in the mood for it. To his surprise when he walked through the door of his home he found the floor covered with red rose petals and candles. All the lights were off and soft music played from the surround sound speakers strategically located around the house.

Wondering what Dylan had up under her sleeve, Angel followed the trail of petals and candles into the dining room. He found Dylan sitting in a chair with nothing but a dark teal, lace, halter style, deep v-neck, teddy. Her full, firm breasts sat up perfectly without any support. Dylan's body was sick. She was thick in all of the right places. Her long, lean legs were covered in bronze, shimmering lotion that sparkled underneath the glow from the candles. In her hand she held a single rose. Angel had never seen a woman look sexier.

"How are you Mr. Carter?" Dylan asked, seductively.

"Better now. What's all of this?" He asked, dropping his gym bag to the floor.

"This is an, I was being a fool for not respecting your feelings, will you forgive me dinner." Dylan stood and escorted him over to his seat then sat on his lap and wrapped her arms around his neck.

"I love you, okay and I'm sorry for putting another man before you. If you don't want me to be friends with State anymore, I won't. It'll just be a hi and bye thing from now on," she said truthfully.

"Thank you," Angel replied, pleased.

"Now can we stop fighting and get back to making love?" Dylan unsnapped the top of her teddy, revealing her luscious breasts.

"You ain't said nothing but a word."

The one thing Billie loved most in her life was her children. The bond that she had with them was unbreakable. Kyrese, Kenzie and Kaylee could talk to her about anything. Billie promised to never judge them but give them sound advice. She particularly loved showering them with unexpected surprises for their good behavior and grades in school. When the kids least expected it Billie would treat them with a fun activity.

It was a sunny Wednesday afternoon and Billie had just picked up Kyrese from middle school. Since they still had an hour and a half to spare before getting the twins, Billie decided to surprise Kyrese with a visit to Game Stop and frozen yogurt at FroYo. Kyrese was ecstatic by the spur of the moment show of affection from his mother. Billie cherished seeing the look of joy on her sons face. Kyrese was getting so big. He was turning into a young man right before her eyes. She just prayed that no matter what came their way he'd continue to love her despite her mistakes.

"What flavor yogurt are you getting," she asked, Kyrese.

"Red velvet cake and I'ma put sprinkles, brownies, strawberries and Fruity Peebles on it," Kyrese answered, gleefully.

"Don't come crying to me when you're stomach start hurting," Billie teased.

"Mama, I am not five. I'll be straight."

"You'll be straight?" Billie arched her eyebrow. "Boy, get outta here. When you become so cool?"

"Mama, you ain't know? I'm that dude," Kyrese stopped and posed.

"Chile, ain't nobody got time for that," Billie giggled, when the store door opened and she spotted State walking in.

A chill so cold she felt frozen in time ran up Billie's spine. Instantly they caught eyes with one another. By the looks on both their faces neither was happy to see the other. Billie was not too pleased to see him with a drop-dead-gorgeous girl who looked to be in her early twenties.

"Mama," Kyrese patted his mother on the arm, ecstatically. "There go State."

"I see baby. C'mon lets go pay for our yogurt before it melts," Billie said, frantically.

"I'm gettin' ready to go say hi," Kyrese responded, making sure his outfit was in tact.

"No!" Billie shrieked. "We're getting ready to go." Billie threw the money for their yogurt at the cashier and grabbed his hand.

"Ma'am, what about your change?" The cashier yelled.

"Keep the change!" Billie shouted back.

"So you just gon' walk past me and not speak?" State questioned.

"Why would I do anything different," Billie remarked, with an attitude.

"What up State?" Kyrese spoke cheerfully.

"What up man?" State gave him a pound and admired his outfit. "I see you. You lookin' fresh. Out here stuntin' like yo' daddy." He said, coyly lookin' Billie directly in the face.

Almost about to have a heart attack Billie shot State an evil glare and said, "C'mon Kyrese. We have to go pick up your sisters."

"Good seeing you State," Kyrese said, as Billie dragged him out of the yogurt shop.

In the car, Billie turned the radio on and the volume up high. She desperately needed something to drown out the erratic thoughts in her head. Her body was so tense and tight that she thought she was going to have a panic attack. Driving down the street without having an accident was even a hard task. She wished that she could pull over and break down and cry but her son was in the car. She had to stay as calm as possible without freaking him out.

Kyrese gazed over his mother. There was no denying that she was a nervous wreck. Her entire body was shaking and she was taking short deep breaths. Billie was driving so fast that Kyrese was afraid they were going to crash. He couldn't understand for the life of him what could've gotten his mother so upset. Then it dawned on him.

Only one thing could make his mother act so out of character. Kyrese had wondered about it for months but never had the guts to say it out loud. Everyday his suspicions grew deeper. He had to know so he could put his fears to rest. Reaching over he turned the volume down on the radio.

"Ah uh, turn that back up," Billie snapped.

"Mama, I gotta ask you a question." Kyrese's voice quivered.

"What is it Kyrese?" Billie replied, not in the mood.

"Is State my daddy?"

Don't come close. You don't even know me. You think you know me.
-SZA, "Teen Spirit"

Chapter 9

Everything around Billie was moving in slow motion. She heard screams, people crying, sirens and shouting but she couldn't move. She was frozen stiff there on the sidewalk. Blood trickled from her forehead and tiny pieces of glass pierced her skin but she was numb to the pain. It was as if she was a corpse and her spirit had left her body. She watched absent-mindedly as the paramedics lifted Kyrese's limp and bloody body onto the gurney and into the ambulance.

He was barely breathing and wasn't conscious. Billie just stood there replaying in her mind Kyrese asking her if State was his father and her taking her eyes off the road and looking at him with terror in her eyes. Her worst nightmare had come true. Billie swore she must've blacked out for a second because the next thing she knew Kyrese screamed, "Mom watch out!"

Billie quickly focused her attention back on the road but it was too late. She couldn't straighten the wheel fast enough. Before she knew she'd done a 360 circle in the middle of the street then crashed into another vehicle. The impact of Billie hitting the car at such a high speed caused Kyrese, who wasn't wearing his seatbelt to go flying through the windshield. His body was catapulted onto the hood of the car.

Billie's head slammed into the steering wheel and she was knocked unconscious for a brief moment. She came to as soon as officers came to remove her from the car. The fist thing Billie saw when she opened her eyes was Kyrese laying unconscious on the hood of the car.

A scream only a mother could scream escaped from her lungs. She wanted to die instantly. She wanted to trade places with Kyrese. What had she done? Had she killed her baby?

As soon as she got out of the car, Billie tried to run over to Kyrese but the paramedics wouldn't allow it. All she could do was stand idly by while they attended to her wounds as she cried. Minutes later she and Kyrese were whisked away to the nearest hospital. Billie sat alone in the waiting room as a team of doctors attended to Kyrese. Hugging herself, Billie rocked back and forth repeating to herself, *it's all my fault*. She didn't care that the people around were staring or might think that she was crazy.

At that point she was. Nothing mattered but the health of her son. She'd surely die if something were to happen to him. Billie was in such a state of shock that she didn't even remember calling Cain and everyone else about the accident. It wasn't until he and his wife Puss-n-Boots came barging into the waiting room demanding answers that she remembered.

"Where is my son?" Cain demanded to know.

"Who is your son sir?" One of the nurses asked.

"Kyrese Townsend."

"He's in the E.R., sir. The doctors are attending to him now." The nurse confirmed.

"His mother was in the accident with him. Is she okay?" Cain questioned.

"Yes sir. Mrs. Christianson only had a few minor wounds. She's right over there in the waiting room." The nurse pointed.

Cain looked over his shoulder at Billie who was still rocking herself. A mixture of sorrow and anger washed over him. He was happy that the mother of his children was okay but he was pissed that she was the cause of his only son being hurt.

"Billie!" Cain rushed by her side. "What the hell happened?" He sat down beside her.

"It's all my fault," Billie repeated again crying.

"That's obvious." Puss-n-Boots shot underneath her breath.

Billie may have been distraught but she still peeped Puss-n-Boots shady comment. Billie instantly stopped rocking and shot her a death glare from hell.

"What happened?" Cain questioned, irritated.

"I took my eyes off the road for a second and crashed the car." Billie spoke almost above a whisper.

Her throat was raw and soar from all of the screaming and crying she'd done.

"Why in the hell would you take your eyes off the road? What could've possibly been that important?" Cain barked.

Billie looked him square in the eyes and swallowed hard. Every since Kyrese was born she'd dreaded this moment. She'd avoided it all cost. Nothing would ever be the same once the truth was revealed. Everyone would see her for who she truly was, which was a monster. Just as Billie closed her eyes and parted her lips to say the words that would change everything Dylan, Tee-Tee, Angel, Bernard and Knox came running into the waiting room. *Thank you Jesus,* Billie thought letting out a sigh of relief.

"Baby, are you alright?" Knox swiftly swooped her up into his arms.

"I'm okay," she said, wincing from the pain of him hugging her too tight. "Oww-oww!" Billie stepped back.

"I'm sorry," Knox cupped her face and kissed her lips. "I'm just happy that you're okay."

"Me too." Angel lightly hugged his sister.

"How is Kyrese?" Dylan asked, worried.

"He's in critical condition." Billie's voice trailed off as the realization that she'd caused harm to her son once again sank in.

"I need to sit down," she said, feeling light headed.

Knox helped his wife ease back into her seat.

"What happened?" Tee-Tee quizzed.

"Can someone please get me some water?" Billie asked, buying herself some more time.

"Sure sweetie." Dylan got up and went over to the vending machine.

Dylan was mortified to see her best friend in such bad shape. Dried up tears and blood adorned Billie's face. Cuts and scrapes were scattered all over her body. She looked as if she'd died a million times. Dylan wished there was something she could do. She felt helpless. For the first time in their friendship, Billie needed her more than ever. Dylan was determined to do whatever she needed in order to help her through this trying time in her life.

"Here you go." Dylan handed Billie the cold bottle of water.

Billie opened the bottle and took a long gulp. Everyone was staring at her, waiting for her to tell the story of how the accident occurred. Billie couldn't handle the pressure. She wanted nothing more than to disappear or drown in the bottle of water.

"Mrs. Christianson?" A doctor approached her.

"Yes," Billie stood up.

"I'm Dr. Kline. I just wanted to give you an update on your sons' condition. He's suffered a head injury and lost a lot of blood. We're going to need to perform a blood transfusion in order to restore the blood that he's lost."

"Of course, take mine." Billie replied, ready to go.

"Mine too." Cain stepped up.

"If you both can follow me." A nurse requested.

Billie and Cain both gave their blood and were bandaged up and back in the waiting room in no time. No one said a word. Everyone inside of the waiting room sat silent, deep in their own thoughts until Dylan spoke up.

"I know that we're all praying for Kyrese but can somebody please tell exactly what happened?" She died to know.

"Who has the girls?" Billie asked, changing the subject.

"Candy, she's watching all of the kids at your house," Tee-Tee responded. "Now how exactly did the accident occur?" He asked again.

Billie examined everyone's face. They were all waiting on pins and needles for her response. Billie once again was under fire. She couldn't physically handle telling them the truth. A rush of anxiety swept over her. It was as if she were having a heart attack. Her heart felt like it had sunk down to the pit of her stomach. Her hands were wet and clammy and each small breath she took felt like it would be her last.

"Billie, are you alright?" Angel, asked, concerned. She was as white as a ghost.

"I can't breathe," she said, holding her chest.

"Do we need to get a doctor?" Knox asked.

"No!" Billie shook her head profusely. "I just need a minute," she said, taking large deep breaths.

"Lord, why is this happening to me?" She wailed.

"Shhhh." Dylan rubbed her back.

"Why is this happening to you?" Cain screwed up his face. "Our son is the one suffering, not you. You're to blame for all of this! If you would've been paying attention to the road none of this would have ever happened," he yelled.

"Ay yo', you need to chill the fuck out," Knox warned. "Can't you see she's going through enough?"

"My son is the one suffering. Whatever she's going through she brought it on herself," Cain shot.

"Wow!" Knox said stunned. "Billie told me you were a cruel muthafucka but damn, dude. You're like Satan."

"Satan ain't got nothing on me when it comes to my kids." Cain seethed with anger.

"Will ya'll stop already?!" Dylan yelled, fed up. "This is not about you. This is about Kyrese. Whatever beef ya'll have is a non-muthafuckin' factor. We have to come together as a family right now and pray for this baby's recovery. Now everybody join hands." Dylan looked around at everyone.

When they didn't move fast enough she screamed, "Now goddamnit!"

Not wanting to piss her off even more everyone joined hands and bowed their heads.

"Dear heavenly father," Dylan began. "Lord, we come to you right now asking that you heal Kyrese. Cover him in your blood, Lord Jesus. Whatever's broken in him we ask that you fix it? We ask that you touch every person that comes in contact with him, hearts and minds. You said that you would bless us with the desires of our hearts. Well God, I'm asking you, we're asking you to wake Kyrese up. Heal him God. In Jesus name I pray, amen." Dylan lifted her head and revealed a face full of tears.

Angel hated to see his wife cry but he understood her pain. His nephew was a few feet away lying on a hospital bed, fighting for his life. The mere thought of it made him sick cause just as easily as it was Kyrese lying unconscious, it could've been Mason. Angel was heartbroken for his sister. He'd never witnessed her so broken and helpless, she barely blinked. All she did was sit staring blankly. He wished he could fix this for her but only God could bring them through this. While they all sat deep in their own thoughts as the doctor reemerged with documents in his hand.

"Mrs. Christianson and Mr. Townsend may I speak to you both for a second." Dr. Kline summoned them.

"Sure." Cain quickly stood up and walked over to the doctor.

Billie swiftly followed suit. As Cain and Billie talked to the doctor everyone sat with baited breath waiting to hear what he had to say. None of them was prepared for what was about to happen.

"What?!" Cain shrilled. "That can't be right!"

"I'm sorry Mr. Townsend but we ran the test multiple times. There is no way possible that you are a match for Kyrese."

"If I'm not a match then that means that he's not my son." Cain furrowed his brows and looked at Billie.

Billie couldn't even give him eye contact.

"Billie!" Cain held her by the arms and shook her. "Tell this man he's made a mistake! Kyrese is my son!" He shook her profusely.

"I'm sorry!" Billie broke down in a heap of tears. "I'm so sorry," she wept.

"Oh my god," Dylan gasped, placing her hand on her chest.

"Chile this here is better than an episode of Scandal!" Tee-Tee popped his lips.

"I know the news is shocking to you sir but we do not condone physical violence. You two have to pull it together for the sake of your son." Dr. Kline ordered.

"Apparently he's not my son." Cain pushed Billie away from him like she was a piece of trash.

Cain felt like a limp rag doll. He'd experienced physical pain on the football field but nothing could compare to the searing pain he felt at that very moment. Nothing or no one could've prepared him for this. Kyrese was his son, his only son. He'd cared him from the second he entered the world. He acted just like him. He wanted to play football just like him and carry-on the family name. How could he not be his son? Most importantly how long had Billie known that he was not his son?"

"Baby, are you alright?" Cain heard Puss-n-Boots ask.

"No." Cain shook his head as a million tears slid down his cheeks.

"Mrs. Christianson?" Dr. Kline turned to her. "For the sake of your son we need to know who Kyrese's father is so we can have a positive match in order to perform the blood transfusion."

Billie was so hysterical that she couldn't even stand up. Her legs felt like Jello. To stand on her own two feet was an impossible fete. Seeing her entire life crumble before her eyes was too much to bear so she fell to her knees asking God to help her.

"Help me father, please," she cried.

"Mrs. Christianson?" Dr. Kline repeated. "We need to know who the father is immediately."

"You need to go help her!" Angel said to Knox.

"I can't," Knox said, frozen stiff.

Hearing the shocking news that Cain wasn't Kyrese's father had him shook. He'd defended Billie when she spoke ill against Cain. She painted him out to be a monster, when all along she was the villain.

"C'mon, we gotta help her." Dylan said, to Tee-Tee.

They both without hesitation rushed to their friend's side.

"Billie, honey." Dylan spoke sweetly. "We need you to tell this man who the father is. Kyrese's life is on the line. You have to tell him." Dylan cupped her face in her hands.

Billie gazed into Dylan's eyes and cried.

"I can't."

"Yes, you can." Dylan assured as Tee-Tee rubbed Billie's back.

"I can't!" Billie's chest heaved up and down. "I'm going to lose you too."

"You would never lose me. We're bffs for life. Hell, fuck being best friends. You're my sister and I love you.

We all make mistakes, honey. I'm the queen of fucking up."

"You got that right." Tee-Tee agreed.

Dylan shot him an evil glare.

"Sorry, wrong time." Tee-Tee raised his hands up in the freeze position.

"Now come on. It's time to act like a big girl. Tell us who the father is so we can get him up here immediately." Dylan wiped away Billie's tears.

Billie gazed down at the floor. She knew that once the words escaped her lips that nothing would ever be the same. She'd lose everyone she loved and who loved her. She'd lied and betrayed them all but none would be more hurt and disappointed than Dylan. She'd betrayed their friendship and the trust that they'd built. As soon as she told the truth there would be no more Billie and Dylan. Their friendship would be over for good.

"Billie you have to tell us who it is?" Dylan looked at her with sympathy in her eyes.

"It's State," Billie whispered.

Within a matter of a half a second the look of sympathy in Dylan's eyes instantly turned to hate.

"What did you say?" Dylan eased back as if Billie was the devil.

"Kyrese's father is State."

"That's not possible. You didn't even know him until we met," Dylan responded confused.

"I've know him since I was twenty-three," Billie sniffed. "Dylan, I'm so sorry." Billie tried to reach for her hand.

"Uh ah," Dylan snatched her hand away. "Why would you make up a lie like that? What the fuck is wrong wit' you?" Dylan asked, heated.

"I wish it was a lie but it's the truth," Billie cried.

"Jesus be a fence!" Tee-Tee placed the back of his hand up to his forehead and fainted.

"Baby!" Bernard caught him mid-faint.

"Does anyone have this State person's contact info?" Dr. Kline looked around.

"Yes, I do," Dylan said, slowly feeling like she was having an outer body experience.

"Dylan, I'm sorry." Billie tried to reach out and hold her hand again.

"Bitch, don't touch me." Dylan's nostrils flared.

A million questions boggled her mind. Dylan looked at Billie, who was drenched in tears. She couldn't even recognize her. Her friend had gone missing. She looked like a monster. She looked like every other person in Dylan's life who had done her wrong. Never would she have expected that Billie, her sister, would be added to the list.

"Here." Dylan handed the doctor her phone.

There was no way she could call State herself. She hadn't even processed the news enough to express the words.

"Dylan, I know I should've told you," Billie pleaded.

"You should've told her?" Cain yelled in disbelief. "How about you should've told me?!"

"I know," Billie screamed, holding her head. "I fucked up! I'ma piece of shit! I should've told all of you!" She wept uncontrollably.

"You damn right you should've!" Cain pointed his finger in her face.

After the explosive news settled in the air the waiting room went dead silent. Everyone was in their perspective corners. Billie sat alone with a wad of tissue in her hand. Knox sat off to the side alone staring at his wife wondering if he'd married a complete stranger. Since the day he'd met Billie he'd been completely open and honest with her about his life.

There was nothing about his life she didn't know. So many nights had gone by where they sat up and talked about their life, their hopes and dreams. She'd never once hinted to the fact that Cain wasn't Kyrese's father. It scared Knox that she could keep such a huge secret for such a long period of time without cracking.

Tee-Tee and Bernard sat in the center of the room holding each other tight. For the first time in a long time, Tee-Tee felt completely safe and secure in him and Bernard's marriage. They'd fought long and hard to have the family they'd built. He would never jeopardize what they had.

As he held Bernard close he looked over at Billie. He honestly felt sorry for her. She looked so afraid. He'd never witnessed her in a more vulnerable state. He wanted to hug her and tell her that everything would be okay but even Tee-Tee wasn't sure of that. Billie had committed the ultimate sin. Nobody except God was ready to forgive her.

Dylan most certainly wasn't ready or willing to forgive her. She couldn't even look at Billie. She despised her. She would never look at her the same again. All of the admiration and trust they'd built over the years had been built upon a lie. Now it made total sense why Billie hated State so much. The hate she pretended to have for him probably was secretly lust.

Dylan stared at Billie and wondered how she and State met. Was it an instant attraction? Had she loved him? Had he loved her? So many thoughts tormented Dylan's mind. She wanted to rip Billie's hair out. She wanted to choke her. Dylan hated her so much she even wanted to spit in her face.

To her Billie was a fake, a fraud, a complete and utter hypocrite. She'd made Dylan look like a fool. For over three years Dylan cried on Billie's shoulder about State. Never once did she open her mouth and say, *'Hey I have a son with the man you love.'* Dylan always secretly looked up to Billie. She was the epitome of grace, elegance and class. In comparison to Billie she always came across dingy and insecure. She always felt inadequate. Billie never ceased to make her feel opposite either.

She always put Dylan down and made her feel less than. Maybe the entire time Billie was jealous that State loved Dylan. Hell, it was obvious that he loved Dylan more than he loved her. Dylan would never forgive Billie. Their over ten year friendship was over. As if things couldn't get anymore complicated, the emergency room doors opened and in walked State.

He was dressed to the nine in a custom made, black Tom Ford tuxedo. A white cashmere scarf hung delicately from his neck. No other man on the planet could rock a suit or a tuxedo like State. The fabric seemed to cling to the peaks and valleys of his muscular physique.

"Sorry it took me so long to get here." He stated out of breath. "I was at a charity gala all the way across town. Now can somebody please explain to me what is going on?"

"You the daddy!" Tee-Tee blurted out carelessly. "Survey says!" He imitated Steve Harvey on the Family Feud. "You're Kyrese's daddy!"

State was every bit the color of black Hawaiian sand but when he learned that he was Kyrese's father he turned the color of snow.

"Billie, is that true?" He glanced over at her helplessly.

The fact that there was no denial of their secret relationship on State's part killed Dylan.
Billie didn't even bother responding to State. Instead she inhaled deeply and rolled her eyes. The response was confirmation for State. He didn't need for her to say yes.

"Now listen." Tee-Tee threw his hips from side to side and sashayed over to State. "Kyrese has lost a lot of blood in the accident and the doctors need you to give up some of your blood so Kyrese can have a C.S.I."

"A what?" State screwed up his face.

"A colonoscopy." Tee-Tee corrected himself.

"What?" State said, confused.

"He needs a blood transfusion," Cain yelled, sizing State up.

"There you go!" Tee-Tee snapped his finger, proudly. Now just scurry your lil' fine self down that hallway to that cute lil' ole nurse and she'll take it from there.

Don't sleep when you know you
gotta good girl.
-Beyoncé feat Drake, "Mine"

Chapter 10

The longer Dylan sat in the emergency room trying to conceal her anger the angrier she became. Every time she looked over at Billie and saw that stupid expression of guilt on her face, she wanted to slap the taste out of her mouth. Everyone was trying to be respectful of her feelings and not bring up the obvious but Dylan was over the silence. If no one else was going to call her out on her shit she was.

"So you just gon' sit there and not say nothing?" Dylan shot. "I mean damn, you owe everyone in this room an explanation."

"I know that I do," Billie said, somberly.

"You know what?" Dylan waved her off. "Save it 'cause the only thing that's going to come out of that mouth is another goddamn lie."

"Lying ass heffa." Dylan rolled her eyes.

"Yo' calm down," Angel grimaced.

"Excuse you?" Dylan turned and looked at him.

"It's too much going on for all that."

"Well excuse the fuck outta me!" Dylan drew her head back, appalled. "Excuse me for fucking having feelings. I just had a freakin' bombshell dropped on me. I'm mad. I'm upset and I have every right to feel some type of way right about now!"

"Nobody said that you shouldn't be upset but you going mighty hard for a nigga you ain't got feelings for!" Angel shot. "Last I checked you were married to me. So why you trippin' off this nigga being Kyrese father?"

"You playing right?" Dylan quizzed. "How would you feel if you were with someone for three years and were engaged to marry them and then you find out that your so called best friend slash sister in-law has not only slept with him but had a whole child with that person? I straight up loved that man. He took me through hell and back and Billie," Dylan pointed her finger in her direction.

"Your sister sat idly by and watched the shit with glee!" Dylan erupted from her seat.

"Seeing you hurt over State never made me happy." Billie tried to explain.

"Bitch fuck you!" Dylan threw up the middle finger. "You probably enjoyed every fuckin' minute of it. Cause you're fuckin' miserable! If yo' ass ain't happy, ain't nobody fuckin' happy!"

"Dylan sit down! You're causing a damn scene." Angel tried to yank her down by her arm.

"I will not calm down! 'Cause somebody need to tell her ass about herself! What kind of person sits there and holds a secret like that for twelve years. I mean this bitch didn't flinch! You sat there and watched me fall in-love with this man and him break my heart, knowing damn well you have fucked him too and he yo' baby daddy!"

"That was pretty ratchet, Billie," Tee-Tee confessed.

"That's some sick shit, right? And poor Cain!" Dylan threw her hands up in the air, frantically. "You have dogged this man from the moment he left you! This man has been every name in the fuckin' book, except a child of god!"

Dylan walked over, leaned down and got Billie's face.

"Uh oh it's... about... to... go... down." Tee-Tee's eyes grew wide.

"You made us hate him. You had us feeling sorry for you when he left you. Now I see why." Dylan seethed with anger.

"I would've left yo' ass too. You're pathetic."Spit spewed from her mouth.

"Ok that's enough!" Angel grabbed her by the arm.

"Oh no! I'm just getting started!" Dylan said, amped up.

"Start yo' ass out of the damn door." Angel pulled her out of the building. "You feel better now?" He let her go once the hospital doors closed.

"No, I don't!" Dylan paced back and forth.

"What the fuck you pacing and shit for? You amped than a muthafucka over this shit, to the point you making me think you still love this nigga." Angel looked her up and down.

"You know what?" Dylan stopped dead in her tracks and looked at him.

"You need to stop! If I wanted to be wit' State, I would fuckin' be with him! You have to get it into your thick ass head that my best friend and fiancé both lied to me! What they did to me is some shit you would see on Maury Povich! This shit ain't normal! My fuckin' feelings are hurt. I'm confused and all you're worried about is you and your insecure ass feelings!"

"Insecure?" Angel furrowed his brows. "I'm far from insecure, ma."

"I can't tell! 'Cause every five seconds you keep bringing up do I still have feelings for him!" Dylan rolled her neck. "You can't put yourself in my shoes and see how I feel?"

"And you don't wanna acknowledge how the fuck I feel!" Angel yelled, causing the veins in his neck to bulge. "Every time I turn around here this nigga come! You cheated on me with this lousy muthafucka! I don't want this nigga nowhere around you or my family!"

"Well too fuckin' late!" Dylan shrugged her shoulders.

"Your sister fucked him too so now he's in our life for good." She reached inside her pocket and grabbed her car keys. "I'm over this shit."

"Where you going?" Angel asked.

"To get my baby and go the fuck home!" Dylan stormed off.

"I rode wit' you! How in the hell am I going to get home?!"

"Ask State to drop you off," Dylan spat.

"You real funny." Angel sucked his teeth then walked back inside.

Just as he reentered the waiting room the doctor reemerged with more news.

"I'm happy to say that State was a match and that the blood transfusion was a success. Kyrese is in stable

126

condition but he still hasn't awakened yet." Dr. Kline stated.

"Thank you god!" Tee-Tee exhaled a sigh of relief.

"Can I go see him?" Billie asked.

"Yes," Dr. Kline smiled.

"I would like to see him too," Cain said too.

"Of course. Follow me." Dr. Kline led the way to Kyrese's hospital room.

A few hours passed and everyone had gone home except Billie. It didn't matter to her that she needed to clean herself up and get some rest. The only thing that mattered was Kyrese. He looked so peaceful as he lay unconscious in the hospital bed. It looked as if he was simply asleep but the fact that he may never wake up lingered over Billie's head. All sorts of tubes were stuck to his body. Billie didn't know how long she could watch him lie in such a helpless, sickly state.

It was especially hard to see him that way knowing that it was her fault he was there. She kept praying to God that he wake up and at least move so that she would know he was alright. But minute after minute nothing happened. He just lie there breathing lifelessly. Every second that went by with him not awake tore at Billie's heart. There was no way on God's green earth that she could lose her son.

He was her everything. When Cain left, he became the man of the house. He helped Billie run the house and keep the twins in line. He was her mini me. Kyrese was reserved and quiet just like her. He spoke only when necessary and when he did it was always something profound and way beyond his years.

"C'mon Kyrese, wake up for mommy," Billie pleaded, holding his hand. "Please just wake up."

But nothing happened. The heart monitor continued to beep and Kyrese just lie there frozen in time. Billie closed her eyes inhaled deeply then exhaled. No amount of money or influence she had would fix this. She couldn't talk her way out of this. Only God could pull Kyrese through and at the moment he seemed to have him on hold. For Billie things couldn't have gotten worse that was until State walked into the room.

"Uh ah!" She shook her head. "Not now. I can't deal with you right now." She shook her head back and forth.

"We all can't get what we want now can we?" State responded, coolly.

"What do you want?"

"I came to see my son. Do you mind?" He replied, sarcastically.

"Actually, I do cause I would prefer some alone time with him."

"You've had twelve years of having him all to yourself. I think it's time you learn how to share." State unbuttoned his tuxedo jacket and pulled up a chair on the opposite side of the bed.

"How in the hell did you keep this shit a secret for all of these years? He looks just like me." State looked on at Kyrese.

"I did what I had to do." Billie stared at Kyrese too.

"You didn't have to what you did, though."

"Oh yes, I did." Billie nodded her head.

"So you knew all along that he was my son?"

"I knew from the moment the pregnancy test said positive," Billie declared.

"So why didn't you ever tell me?"

"You're kidding me right?" Billie looked at him like he was stupid.

"Does it look like I'm playing?" State ice grilled her.

"You must have selective amnesia." Billie shot with an attitude.

"What are you talking about?" State asked confused.

Billie's heart began to race a mile a minute thinking about her and State's past. Twelve years had passed but she could remember every moment they shared as if it were yesterday. She was twenty-three years old and fresh on summer break from school. Billie was beyond excited to begin her summer internship at a budding record company called Mass Appeal. The record label had only been active two years and had already signed five major artists, two of which had gone diamond. Mass Appeal was a great place for Billie to get her feet wet in the music industry.

Her mother Cissy highly disapproved of her decision. She felt that Billie should have been in New York interning at the Guggenheim or in Florence, Italy at the Galleria Dell'Accademia not at some hip hop and r&b record label in St. Louis. But for the first time in her life, Billie decided to defy her mother and do what made her happy. Her entire life she'd lived for her mother. Anything Cissy wanted, Billie did. She had to be the perfect, pristine daughter.

Angel on the other hand got to be free and do as he pleased because he was a boy, which Billie never understood. When Angel decided he wanted to become a professional boxer there was no dispute. Their parents found him the best trainer money could buy and from there his career soared. When Billie expressed her feelings about going into the music industry to become an industry exec her parents, especially her mother flipped.

She told Billie that no respectable woman as smart as Billie should work in the music industry. To Cissy the music industry was filled with a bunch of crooks, gang bangers and drug dealers. Cissy wanted Billie to follow in her and every other socialites' footsteps. She thought Billie should graduate from college, marry well, have children, become philanthropic, throw lavish parties and support her husbands' dreams. Although Billie loved Cain her boyfriend and high school sweetheart she saw herself as more than a football player's future wife. She had dreams all her own that she wanted to fulfill. Despite her mothers' disapproval Billie was determined to spend the summer doing what made her happy.

Besides, Cain was off in Texas in training camp and she would only get to see him every other weekend. She really didn't have that many friends except for Dylan and

Dylan was off in L.A. trying to become an actress. That left Billie alone for the summer. Her first week at Mass Appeal was nothing short of hectic and chaotic. Every other second she was running errands and butting heads with a fellow intern named State.

He was British, handsome as hell, cocky as fuck and took every opportunity he could to get under Billie's skin. Billie knew that underneath all of the bickering was an underlining mutual attraction but she wasn't going to cross the line. State was a player and she loved Cain. In a few years they would be married and living in Texas. She wasn't going to let some annoying Brit side track her plans. But one day as they worked late on a project, neither could hide their feelings any longer.

Right there in the empty office building Billie and State succumb to passion. The affair went on for weeks. Each encounter was better than the last and before Billie knew it she was head over heels in-love with State. Despite his wandering eye, she couldn't stop her feelings from growing. Yes, she knew that he was no-good but with her he showed a different side of his self. Many of nights passed where they discussed his childhood in Hackney London.

He revealed that his father was a deadbeat that barely took care of him and his brothers. State's father was a serial cheater who didn't come home most nights. He expressed his fear of ending up like his father. He told her how afraid he was of failure and not reaching his goals. They both learned that they had a mutual love for the arts. He told her of his dream of one day owning his own label and becoming the hip hop Berry Gordy. State never revealed or shared so much of his self with anyone else. Billie felt special.

When they made love she could see the look of love in his eyes. She felt it every time they touched. Billie had never felt the way she felt for State for Cain. State was falling for her but deep down he knew that what they shared would never last. He wasn't ready for a commitment. Although he loved Billie he couldn't see himself settling down with her at such a young age. Neither of them had ever felt a connection so strong with anyone else but the timing just wasn't right.

After weeks of secretly dating and hooking up Billie became pregnant. She wasn't even shocked by the news because she and State had stopped using protection soon after their affair began. She was 100% sure the baby was State's because she and Cain only slept together every few weeks. Billie and State had been fucking non-stop all summer long. Billie was thrilled. Learning that she was pregnant was the confirmation she'd been searching for.

For weeks she'd been contemplating breaking up with Cain. She didn't love him the way she did State. Cain didn't make her feel alive. With him it was always a safe, sure thing. With State everything was spur of the moment and adventurous. The day she was going to tell State she was pregnant was one of the worst days of Billie's life. She'd been searching for him all over the office building. When she finally found him, she spotted him coming out of the women's restroom zipping up his pants.

Billie was thoroughly confused as to why he would be using the women's restroom until she saw their boss Aneese come out a few seconds later, looking disheveled and satisfied. Billie's heart sank to the floor. She'd never been so hurt in her entire life. When she confronted State on it, he hit her with the famous *"you're not my girl"* line and kept it moving like she wasn't shit. After that there was no way she was going to tell him she was pregnant with his baby.

Her only choice was to have an abortion so Billie went to the only person she could lean on during the time, her mother. Cissy was disappointed and distraught over the news. She couldn't believe that her beautiful, smart, daughter could be so naive and careless. For Cissy, having an abortion wasn't an option. No, Billie would use her pregnancy to her advantage. Cissy came up with the genius idea that Billie would pass the baby off as Cain's to ensure that marriage was in their future.

Billie was disgusted by her mothers' plan but with the threat of being disowned if she aborted the baby looming over her head, she had no choice but to go along with the plan. Once again, Billie found herself living her life for her mother. Shortly after telling Cain she was pregnant they were married. Billie never spoke to State again. Once the internship was over he moved to New York and didn't come back to St. Louis until many years later. Billie and her mother pretended that the lie they created was real. Billie had actually convinced herself that Kyrese was Cain's son until Kyrese began to question things. Now here they was years later watching on as their son fought for his life.

"So you're going to sit up here and pretend like I didn't catch you fuckin' Aneese? When I called you out on it you gave me your ass to kiss." Billie's voice cracked.

"Billie what did you want from me? I was young and I was selfish. I only did it because I knew that I could never be what you wanted me to be. I cared about you a lot but at the time I was trying to make it by any means necessary and loving you wasn't a part of the equation," State confessed.

"So why not say that instead of ripping my heart out of my chest?" Billie teared up.

"I was a coward. I didn't want to see you look at me the way you're looking at me right now."

Billie swallowed back the tears in her throat and sat up straight. Her life was once again a mess. This time, playing make-believe and lying wasn't going to fix anything. She had to face the reality that from that day forward life would never be the same.

I don't wanna argue, be angry no more.
-Justine Skye, "Good By Now"

Chapter 11

Angel didn't know what kind of environment he was going to walk into as she placed his key in the door. The way Dylan left the hospital he wasn't sure if she'd still be on a rampage or not. In all the years he'd known her, he'd never seen her so belligerent. She'd never come at him the way she had that day. They always talked in calm tones and tried to respect each others feelings. Sometimes things would escalate but never to the point of flat out disrespect.

He thought they'd gotten past the whole State situation after their talk but now with the news that he and Billie were past lovers revealed, a whole new crop of emotions spilled onto the surface. State was like a roach that just wouldn't die. No matter how many times Angels tried to step on him and kill him, he kept on scurrying. He was the thorn in his side. He'd caused the two women Angel loved most extreme heartache.

The dude was bad news. Nothing but trouble came along with him and for some reason Dylan couldn't see it. It seemed to Angel that she was madder at Billie than State. Maybe she had a right to be but State still played a major role in her pain as well. Angel placed his keys down on the stand by the door and made his way to their bedroom.

On his way there, he found Dylan quietly tip toeing out of Mason's room. It was apparent that she'd just finished putting him to sleep. As Dylan closed Mason's door behind her, she jumped at the sight of Angel. She hadn't heard him come in. Once she calmed down from the initial shock, she inhaled deep, rolled her eyes and strolled right past as if he didn't exist.

"So you just gon' walk past me like you don't see me?" Angel smirked, following her into their bedroom.

"Yep," Dylan replied, bluntly.

She was still pissed as hell. She didn't have the time or the energy to argue with Angel. She'd fed, bathed and put her baby to sleep. She was going to shower and get ready for bed herself and ignore the fuck outta him.

"Oh so you call yourself still being mad?" He took off his jacket and threw it onto the bed.

"Umm, can you hang your jacket up?" Dylan ignored his snide comment.

"Sure mother," Angel joked, to get underneath her skin.

Dylan paused and shot Angel a look that could kill.

"Don't play with me." She rolled her eyes hard then went into her walk-in closet to grab a pair of pajamas.

"You need to chill out man and just to let you know the blood transfusion was a success but Kyrese still hasn't woke up yet."

"That's good to know. I pray he wakes up soon. All we can do at this point is to continue to pray for him," Dylan said, sincerely but in a dry tone.

"I'm getting ready to take a shower." She headed towards the bathroom.

"Hold up." Angel pulled her back by the arm. "Let me holla at you for a second."

"I am not about to argue wit' you," Dylan huffed. "I'm tired of being angry and fighting over stupid shit."

"I don't wanna argue wit' you either." He pulled her in close to him.

Angel lovingly placed his arms around Dylan's waist and kissed her on the forehead.

"You know I don't like to see you upset—"

"Stop making me upset then." Dylan cut him off.

"It's not that I'm trying to be mean or nothing. I'm just sick of this dude coming between us. It seems, like every time this nigga name come up it's a bunch of bullshit behind it. Every time we fight it's about him. I'm tired of this nigga causing my family pain," Angel explained.

"But this time it's just not him. It's your sister as well. I'm honestly just over the entire situation. I have been mentally fucked today. I just wanna lie down and go to sleep."

"I know baby." Angel kissed her again.

"I'm sorry you're in pain and if it was up to me I would take it all away. Like straight up, what my sister did was hella fucked up. I can't believe she even did that shit but we can't let her fuck up what we got. We've been through too much shit already and I ain't letting shit come between us. You my baby and I love you." He rocked her back and forth.

"I love you too." Dylan squeezed him tight and closed her eyes.

She wanted more than anything to wish the day away. She wished the accident would have never happened, that Kyrese would've never been hurt, that her over ten year friendship wasn't over and that her heart wouldn't have gotten stepped on with six inch stilettos. Everything was fucked up. Drake was right. Nothing would ever be the same. The dynamic of her life was ruined and deep within

Dylan's heart she knew that things were only going to get worse.

It had been days since Billie had really ate or slept. She hadn't left the hospital except once and that was only for little over an hour just so she could shower and dress. She spent every waking moment at the hospital with Kyrese. Every day and every night she sat by his side watching over him and praying that he woke up. He was breathing on his own but he still hadn't opened his eyes. Her body ached from hardly eating. She felt delirious for not sleeping but none of that mattered to her.

She would trade food and sleep any day just for the gift of Kyrese opening his eyes and calling out her name. But he hadn't and every day another piece of her died. Billie was dying. All she had was herself, really. Tee-Tee, Angel and her mother were the only people worried about her well being. She hadn't heard from Dylan. It hurt like hell to not hear from her but Billie knew that Angel was keeping her updated on Kyrese's condition.

She needed her friend desperately but she understood that she'd done Dylan wrong. Time had to pass before she reached out to her and tried to make things right. No amount of sorry was going to fix it right then. Time would be the only thing to heal the wound. When Cain came to the hospital to visit Kyrese, he didn't speak one single word to her. He acted as if she didn't even exist.

Billie, ironically welcomed him acting like she was invisible. What was she honestly going to say to him anyway? She'd destroyed the mans' life. It was the same with Knox when he came to the hospital. Billie hadn't even really been talking to her own husband. Conversations between them were awkward and strained. When Knox wasn't at the hospital with her, he was at home with the girls.

On that particular day he'd come to bring her lunch and for over two hours they'd sat in silence. Billie sat reading a stack of magazines while Knox sat asleep in a chair. Neither one of them wanted to be the one to say it but their marriage was doomed. The trust had been broken. Knox no longer looked at her the same. She was a complete and utter stranger to him now.

He'd never in a million years think that she'd do something so cruel to so many people she so called loved. The fact that she could so easily with hold the truth for so long frighten him. Knox awoke from his nap and glared at his watch. It was almost time for the girls to get out of school.

"I'm getting ready to go." He cleared his throat while rubbing his eyes.

"Okay." Billie looked up from that month's issue of Vogue magazine. "Tell the girls I love them and that I'll be home tonight to put them to bed."

"Alright." Knox stood up and stretched.

"Thank you again for helping me with the girls."

"No problem." Knox walked to the door.

Normally, he would've kissed Billie goodbye but being sweet and endearing just wouldn't seem natural. Billie wanted him to kiss her or at least give her a hug but she knew if he did it would come across forced. Having him fake intimacy with her would only make her feel ten times worse.

"I'll see you in a few hours," she reconfirmed. "Oh and please make sure that Kaylee and Kenzie eat something healthy tonight. They told me that they've been eating nothing but fast food all week."

"Well, I've been doing the best that I can Billie. I have a lot on my plate too with work, taking care of the girls, coming to the hospital and making sure the house is straight," Knox said, annoyed.

"I wasn't trying to be funny or anything," Billie assured.

"It sure seemed like it," Knox responded, coolly.

"Are we going to be okay?" Billie asked, unsure.

"I don't know," Knox shook his head, massaging his jaw. "I don't know."

All you ever did was wreck me.
-Miley Cyrus, "Wrecking Ball"

Chapter 12

"Girl, I still can't get over the news, honey." Candy sat down at the kitchen island at Tee-Tee's house.

"Me either." Dylan sipped on her glass of ice cold Canada Dry Ginger Ale and examined her mother.

It was a Tuesday afternoon and she was dressed like she was headed to the club. Candy loved to show off her figure. If it wasn't tight it wasn't right. Candy was well into her fifty's and was wearing a green, mesh, cut-out, open back, midi dress with lucite, six inch, stripper heels. Dylan didn't know whether to be impressed that her mother had the body to pull such a look off or appalled that her mother would wear such an outfit on a Tuesday afternoon.

"When she said it, I literally passed out," Tee-Tee laughed.

"I had to help his big ass up," Dylan giggled. "I mean everyone was in shock."

"Who would've thought Billie and State would've bumped uglies." Candy screwed up her face.

"Most certainly not me.Dylan pursed her hips.

"So now that it's settled in some, how do you feel?" Tee-Tee asked as Kenzie and Kaylee ran around in the living room.

He was watching them for Knox while he was at work. Dylan inhaled deep and rolled her eyes.

"I'm angry, I'm disappointed, I'm confused, I'm in shock. There are so many different emotions going through me. I mean, I still don't know how it all went down between the two of them."

"I asked her." Tee-Tee snapped his fingers. "And she spilled the whole tea to me." He popped his lips.

Dylan simply looked at him and arched her eyebrow. She wasn't in the mood for Tee-Tee's over the top dramatic behavior or his brightly colored outfit. She couldn't figure out who looked more of a mess; him or her mother. Tee-Tee was serving Amber Rose realness with his blonde buzz cut, neon yellow camisole displaying his full set of double D breast implants, galaxy garter leggings and hot pink patent leather pumps. There was no way she could take him serious in that get-up.

"What she say?" Dylan cocked her head to the side and prepared herself for the worst.

"Basically, they met back when you were in L.A. trying to be the next Linda Lovelace," Tee-Tee joked.

148

"Umm excuse you. I almost landed a role playing a crackhead in one of Tyler Perry's movies. She," Dylan spoke in third person. "was a great actress." Dylan flipped her imaginary long hair.

"Girl, I could've played a crackhead in one of Tyler Perry's movies. That ain't shit." Tee-Tee waved her off.

"Now back to the tea, bitch. Where was I?" He looked up towards the ceiling.

"Oh yeah, so you were in L.A. and me and her weren't cool yet. It was during the summer and she and State were both interning at Mass Appeal records. They had like this love/hate relationship that apparently flipped into more love than hate and plenty of back breaking. She thought he was the one honey until she found out she was pregnant wit' Kyrese and found him fucking they boss in the women's restroom!" Tee-Tee slapped his hand down on the island for dramatic effect.

"Get the fuck outta here!" Dylan gasped.

"Yes chile and when she confronted him, he hit her with the ole we ain't together line."

"Wow… that's cold-blooded." Candy's eyes grew wide. "So she and Cain were together during this time, right?"

"Mmm hmm," Tee-Tee pursed his lips together. "He was in training camp in Texas. This was when he played for the Dallas Cowboys. They were doing the long distance thing. She would fly down to see him every other weekend."

"So Billie was dropping that thun-thun-thun down on two niggas at the same damn time! Now that's my kinda girl!" Candy clapped her hands and shimmied in her seat.

"Ah uh girl." Candy's boo Clyde danced into the kitchen. "Don't you drop that thang without me!" He grinded his hips.

"Oh my god," Dylan looked up at the ceiling. "Kill me now Jesus."

She'd grown to love her mother's current boo thang but Clyde's permed hair, nappy chest hair, pot belly and 70's attire was just too much for her to bear at times. He was no taller than Kevin Hart and always had on some outdated inappropriate shit. The muddy brown, floral print, flared collar shirt and white, skin tight, bell bottom bibs he wore was a sight for sore eyes. He and her mother together were like watching a bad, over-sexualized rerun of Soul Train.

"How's my baby-mama doing?" Clyde kissed Candy on the tip of her nose and grabbed a chunk full of her ass.

"Boy, don't call me that," Candy grinned like a school girl.

"But you are my baby-mama and I'm your baby-daddy and this is our baby-baby," Clyde draped his arm around Dylan's shoulder.

"If you don't get the hell away from me lookin' like a goddamn D battery." Dylan hissed not in the mood for Clyde's antics.

"Oh that's how it is, Dylan?" Clyde said, stunned. "You think you nickel slick but I got yo' penny change."

"Out!" Dylan shouted, pointing towards the door.

"I've been thrown out better. Sugafoot, I'll be in the living room." Clyde winked his at Candy then left out.

"Anyway … back to our conversation," Dylan crossed her legs. "It just fucks me up how for years she condom me for all of my mistakes—"

"Condemned, sweetie. It's condemned." Tee-Tee patted her on the back of her hand.

"Oh what the fuck ever. Condom, condemned it's all the same thing." Dylan waved her hands frantically.

"Like I was saying. For years she condemned," Dylan stressed the word. "me for making fucked up mistakes but here she had made the ultimate no-no. She cheated on her then boyfriend, gotten pregnant by another dude, lied to Cain and made him believe that the baby was his, then years later sat idly by and watched her best friend date the same man she'd cheated with and had a baby wit'."

"I keep hearing you talk about what Billie did but what about State?" Candy quizzed. "He lied to you too."

"I'm more pissed at Billie because she was supposed to be my friend. Hell, she was like a sister to me. I never thought she'd do something like this to me." Dylan's eyes welled up with tears.

"I trusted her with all of me. She stopped talking to me for damn near a year when I cheated on Angel with State and she knew the whole time that she had a baby with this man." Dylan wiped her face.

"Yeah, that was fucked up," Tee-Tee agreed.

"I mean, State gon' be State. I'm not saying its okay but I don't expect much from him," Dylan sniffled.

"That's sad." Tee-Tee shook his head.

"Ain't it?" Dylan said, somberly.

"Girl, you gotta learn how to shut your feelings off,' Candy advised. "I am an active member of the not many fucks given coalition."

"Tee-Tee!" Kaylee ran into the kitchen.

"Yes, sweetie," Tee-Tee looked loving at the little girl.

Billie's twin daughters were the absolutely cutest things on earth outside of Tee-Tee's daughter. They both looked like two little Bratz dolls. Their little almond shaped and pouty lips were everything and more.

"Can me and Kenzie have some juice?" Kaylee asked, sweetly.

"Sure boo kitten." Tee-Tee got up from the island and opened the fridge.

"We are parched." Kenzie came into the kitchen with her hand up to her throat to emphasize her words.

"Yes, we have worked up a sweet, chile." Kaylee slapped fives with her sister.

Dylan couldn't do anything but laugh at the twins. They were too damn grown for their own good but when she looked at their adorable little faces her heart instantly melted.

"Auntie Dylan!" Kenzie called out for Dylan.

"Yes, baby." Dylan tried to pull herself together so the girls wouldn't notice her tears.

"Why are you crying?"

"Auntie's just a little sad right now."

"Is it because of my ratchet ass mama?" Kenzie placed her hand on her invisible hip.

"Kenzie watch your mouth!" Dylan yelled, caught off guard by her sassiness.

"Well, don't get mad at her." Kaylee took up for her sister. "That's what we heard you call her the other day."

"You don't repeat what you hear grown folks say." Tee-Tee handed them both a juice box.

"All we wanna know is Cain our daddy or nah?" Kenzie spoke in a ghetto girl tone. "Cause we got a funny feeling Gucci Mane might be our daddy."

"If you don't get yo' lil' ass up outta here!" Tee-Tee shooed them out of the kitchen.

"We have a right to know!" Kaylee yelled over her shoulder.

"And you got the right to get my foot up yo' ass! I ain't ya' damn mama! Now go sit down and watch television like normal lil' girls!" Tee-Tee shouted, bewildered.

"They lil' bad asses gon' give me a damn heart attack."

"Now that I think of it Kenzie and Kaylee are kind of crazy as hell." Dylan pondered out loud. "Maybe Gucci is they daddy."

"Girl, if you don't shut up." Tee-Tee laughed, throwing a towel at her face.

Over two weeks had gone by and Kyrese's condition hadn't progressed. He continued to lie in a deep sleep that he seemed to not want to wake from. The longer he stayed unconscious, the more Billie began to deteriorate. She was growing thinner by the day. Not eating or sleeping was making her cranky and irritable. She snapped on the doctors, the nurses, Knox, Cain and State. She didn't want anyone near her son but her.

The waiting game of waiting for Kyrese to awake was physically and mentally killing her. She was losing her mind. Billie didn't know how much more she could take. The sound of the heart monitor was driving her insane. God wasn't answering her call. Maybe this was his way of punishing her for all of the deceit she'd caused. She couldn't blame him. She deserved every rotten thing that came her way but she didn't want Kyrese to suffer for her transgressions. He deserved to live, to be happy and healthy. Billie was the one who should've lay unconscious.

"Please Lord, please. Wake him up," she pleaded, staring at Kyrese.

As she sat there lookin on at him, the door to his room opened. Billie gazed over her shoulder and saw a short, older, white gentleman walk into the room.

"Yes, may I help you?"

"Billie Christian?" The man asked.

"Yes." Billie eyed him.

"Here you go." He handed her an envelope.

"What is this?" Billie took the envelope from his hand.

"You've been served. Have a good day." The man left the room as quick as he came in.

Billie took the envelope. She couldn't imagine who would be trying to take her to court or better yet sue her. Maybe it was the driver of the car she'd hit in the accident. Billie unfolded the papers and read the letter. Halfway through the letter she felt faint. At any second she was sure her heart was going to stop beating and she would be dead.

Cain was ordering an emergency hearing in court the next day to establish full custody of the girls and to relinquish his parental rights to Kyrese. Billie never saw this coming. She never in a million years thought that Cain would so something so cruel but he had and she wasn't prepared. She wasn't in the right frame of mind to battle him in court and he knew that.

"What am I going to do?" Billie said, out loud as the papers slid through her hand and down to the floor.

"Mama," Kyrese spoke groggily, opening his eyes.

"Oh my god!" Billie jumped up. "Mama's here, baby." Billie leaned down and kissed his face.

"My head hurts," Kyrese groaned.

"I know baby." Billie kissed him again. "Can I get a doctor in here," she screamed.

It was one of those lazy Monday's where all Dylan and Angel wanted to do was lay in bed, wrapped up in each others arms. Dylan could honestly lie there staring into his hypnotic eyes till the day she died. She and Angel rarely had moments like these. They were always on the go. They hardly ever got to enjoy each others company and connect on a deeper level. All they had were stolen kisses, quick romps in hidden places and small conversations.

She was thoroughly relishing in lying face to face with her handsome husband. He was everything that she's prayed for and more. No other man on the planet had ever taken the time to love her the way he had. Her happiness was all that mattered to him. Every chance he got he let her know how perfect and beautiful she was to him. She was his girl. Nothing would change that.

Dylan planned on growing old and gray with Angel. He was her king, her protector, her lover and her best friend. All she wanted was to give every piece of her to him. He'd earned it. There under the covers, they lie wrapped up in each others arms listening to Jordan Rakei. The words to his song *Run Away* described how she felt in that very instance. Dylan ran her hand softly down the side of Angel's face. She could never see them falling apart. If they did she would surely die. Outside of Mason, she'd never loved anyone more. Loving him was so easy. Dylan gazed into his eyes and smiled brightly.

"What you smiling at?" Angel yawned and laughed at the same time.

"You nigga." Dylan giggled.

"What you smiling at me for?"

"Cause I am." Dylan bucked her eyes.

"Don't make that face. You look like that ugly ass girl from Facebook you went to school wit'." He joked.

"Eww, no the fuck I don't." She playfully hit him on the arm.

"You know you look like that girl," Angel chuckled.

"Whatever." Dylan waved him off.

"Nah, you know you're the shit." Angel leaned forward and brushed his nose against hers.

There wasn't anything he wouldn't do for her. She was the love of his life. He would walk through fire for her. Waking up each morning knowing that she was there by his side was the best blessing he could receive from god. They'd been through hell and back together. If he did have to serve time for assaulting Javier, he wasn't worried about Dylan straying. He knew that no matter what she'd always be there for him.

He hoped and prayed that he could settle out of court but by the way things were looking Javier and his lawyers were aiming for jail time and a pay off. Angel hadn't told Dylan how serious things had gotten with the case. He didn't want to scare her anymore than she already was. Plus they had enough on their plate as it was. There was no way Angel could go to jail. Right now his family needed him the most.

"Yeah, staying in your apartment ain't where it's at," Angel agreed.

"We need more space and Mason needs a backyard to play in and I was thinking," Dylan smiled, wickedly.

"Oh lord, what?" Angel scratched his head.

"I was thinking that maybe we could start on making baby number two," Dylan said, with an innocent look on her face.

"You out yo' muthafuckin' mind," Angel replied, indignantly.

"What?" Dylan asked, visibly hurt.

"I'm just playing." Angel kissed her all over her face.

"Boy, I was getting ready to say." Dylan welcomed his kisses relieved.

"I really want a girl," Dylan whispered.

"I know you do so you and my sister can spoil the fuck outta her."

"I don't know about that." Dylan immediately became tense.

"Damn, my bad. I forgot," Angel apologized as his phone rang.

"Noooooo don't answer it," Dylan pleaded, pulling him away from his phone.

160

"It's my sister. I gotta answer it. Hello?" Angel sat up.

"Angel," Billie said, excitedly.

"What's up? You a'ight?"

"I'm better than okay," Billie said, barely able to breathe. "Kyrese woke up!"

Angel turned and told Dylan.

"Thank god." Dylan replied, relieved.

"Is he okay?" Angel asked.

"Yes, he has a headache but the doctors say he'll be able to go home in a few days to ensure he's a hundred percent."

"That's good. I'm happy for you Billie."

"Thank you but I also have some bad news." Her voice trailed off.

"What is it?" Angel responded, alarmed.

"Cain is taking me to court tomorrow for an emergency hearing to gain custody of full custody of the girls and to terminate his parental rights to Kyrese."

"What the fuck? So he doesn't want to be Kyrese's father anymore? He's the only dad he knows!" Angel yelled, pissed.

"Are you serious?" Dylan scrunched up her forehead.

161

"Yeah, this nigga straight trying to take the girls away from Billie and relinquish his parental rights for Kyrese."

"Wooooow," Dylan said, stunned.

"Man, fuck that. I'm about to go see this nigga." Angel threw the covers back.

"No!" Billie shouted. "Don't do that. I don't need anything to happen that's going to make me look worse than I already do."

"You're right." Angel calmed down.

"Can you put me on speaker phone for a minute?" Billie asked.

"Yeah, hold on." Angel took the phone away from his ear. "Billie, you there?" Angel spoke into the phone.

"Yeah, I'm here," she answered. "Dylan, hi. How are you?"

"I'm okay." Dylan immediately caught an attitude upon hearing her voice.

"I hate to ask this of either of you but I need both of you to testify on my behalf tomorrow. I can not have my girls taken away from me." Billie's voice trembled.

"We got you." Angel confirmed before Dylan had the chance to respond.

"We do?" Dylan objected.

"Yes, we do." Angel spoke in a stern tone.

"Dylan," Billie interjected. "I know you're upset with me and I am so sorry for all of the pain that I have caused you. But I really need you right now. You know that my kids are everything to me. I can't lose them."

Dylan swallowed hard. Every part of her wanted to be on some fuck Billie type shit but her heart just wouldn't allow it. The kids were the innocent ones in all of the drama their mother had caused. Dylan wasn't feeling Billie at all but even at her maddest she couldn't deny how good of a mother Billie was to her kids. She deserved a lot of foul shit to happen to her but not that.

"I'll be there," Dylan groaned, plopping back onto the bed.

I can't live a lie.
-Miley Cyrus, "Wrecking Ball"

Chapter 13

Billie hated that she had to leave Kyrese for even one second now that he was awake. But there was no way she was just going to sit idly by and let Cain take away her girls without a fight. The kids were her whole entire world. Without them she didn't exist. She'd centered her whole life around them. She'd done her best to be the best mother possible and because of one mistake and one lie, Cain might gain custody. The emergency hearing at the downtown St. Louis courthouse was private.

Only herself, Cain, Puss-n-Boots, their lawyers and the stenographer were in the room. Knox was at work and couldn't take time off so that left Billie all alone. She was overcome with nervousness. Her palms were sweaty, she kept having mini hot flashes, her throat was dry and butterflies filled the pit of her stomach. She didn't know where Angel and Dylan were. She prayed that they wouldn't play her and not show up. She needed all of the support she could get.

Billie couldn't wait for the hearing to be over so she could get back to her son. He needed her and Cain knew that. She couldn't understand why he would be so cruel as to request giving up his parental rights to Kyrese. He was the only father Kyrese knew. How was Billie going to explain to him that his dad didn't want to be his father any longer? It was all too much for Billie to digest.

She would give anything for a Xanax at that moment to calm her nerves but the bailiff had announced the judges' presence and the hearing had begun. Billie swallowed the gigantic lump in her throat and arose from her seat. As Judge Wallace sat down, he requested that everyone else be seated. Billie did as she was told and looked back to see if Angel and Dylan had come in yet. They hadn't.

Inhaling deeply, she concentrated on breathing so she wouldn't pass out. Cain's lawyer began the hearing spewing vile, vicious lies about Billie being an unfit mother. Cain's lawyer depicted her as a self-centered, ego maniac, liar that lived a double life. He told the judge that she was barely at home, a narcissist, a psycho and needed clinical help. Billie expected for Cain to play dirty but not this dirty.

He was making her out to be a monster. She knew that Cain was upset with her. He had every right to be but she didn't deserve for him to come out swinging like they were in a boxing match. Once Cain's lawyer was done tarnishing her character it was Billie's lawyer's turn. As her lawyer rose to tell their side of the case, Angel and Dylan walked in. Billie was relieved to see their faces as they sat behind her.

Billie's lawyer, Todd, told the truth that she was a dedicated, loving, caring mother who put her children before herself. He confirmed that she'd made a mistake lying about Cain being Kyrese's father but that she was young at the time and afraid. Her lawyer told the judge that if Cain wanted to end his parental responsibilities for Kyrese then so be it but he had no grounds to try to gain full custody of Kenzie and Kaylee. Cain was often out of town on business and Puss-n- Boots was in no shape or form fit to be anybody's mother.

As her lawyer spoke Billie looked over at Cain. He sat with a smug look on his face. He was emotionless as always. Billie tried to make eye contact with him but he wouldn't even look her way. She wished they could stop the whole hearing and talk like two adults but Cain wasn't mature enough. He'd been waiting for years to get his digs into Billie. After her lawyer was done speaking on Billie's behalf it was now Cain and Billie's chance to speak. Cain got to go first.

"Your honor." He stood up and straightened his tie.

"I'm here today for the well being of my children. My daughters are not safe with this woman. She's not only a liar but a manipulator and a sociopath. I strongly believe that she needs a clinical evaluation. For years she has made me believe that Kyrese was my son and the only reason why I learned the truth is because of her negligent behavior. My ex-wife caused an automobile accident that nearly killed him and put him in a coma for over two weeks." Cain turned and looked at Billie with disgust.

"Your honor, I do not trust her to be honest, trustworthy or responsible for our daughters anymore."

"And why after raising Kyrese as your own for twelve years do you wish to terminate your parental rights?" Judge Wallace questioned. "Have you thought of how this will affect the boy?"

"Yes, I have and I think that it's best for everyone if Kyrese builds a relationship with his real father." Cain emphasized the word father as he glared at Billie.

"I have never really had a connection with him like I have with my girls and now I know why. We had no connection 'cause he's not my son. I don't want the financial or emotional burden of raising a child that isn't mine. His parents should be responsible for that." Cain once again cut his eyes at Billie before sitting down.

"Mrs. Christianson, it's your turn to speak." Judge Wallace nodded his head towards her.

Billie slowly and weakly rose from her seat. Her entire body shook with fear. All of her life she'd been a fighter but with everything in her life crashing down around her all of her will to win was lost. She didn't want to fight anymore. She was tired of living a lie and making others suffer for it.

"Your honor," Billie's voice cracked. "I didn't mean for any of this to happen. I didn't mean to hurt my son. The accident was just that, an accident. I took my eyes off of the road for a second because I was caught off guard." Her voice quivered.

"I really didn't mean to hurt Cain or anyone else for that matter. I was young and I made a stupid choice that held life long ramifications that I wasn't prepared for at the time. But that's what it was your honor, one mistake. I'm a good mother and I love my children with all of my heart. They will attest to that. I am with my children everyday. Cain is always gone. He's never present even when he's

169

with the kids. Your honor, I can't lose my babies. I can't lose my girls. Now if Cain no longer wants to be Kyrese's father then I won't stand in his way. Kyrese deserves to have a father in his life that truly loves him and will never leave him. It will be hard but I will get him through it." Billie's eyes welled up with tears.

"Just please don't take away my girls. I need them just as much as they need me." Billie pleaded to the judge once more before retaking her seat.

After her plead to the judge, Billie naturally assumed that Judge Wallace would call on their witnesses but he didn't. Judge Wallace went straight into his ruling instead. Billie was stunned. She'd banked on Angel and Dylan's testimony. All she could do now was pray that her lawyers' argument and her testimony would be good enough.

"After careful consideration, I have decided to grant Mr. Townsend's wish to terminate parental custody of Kyrese Townsend as well as gain full custody of Kenzie and Kaylee Townsend."

"Nooooooo!" Billie's heart stopped. "No!" She yelled.

"Billie, you have to calm down." Her lawyer took her hand and tried to calm her down.

"I can't calm down! They're taking away my girls!"
She wailed.

"Mr. Evans, please contain your client," Judge
Wallace warned.

"Your honor, you can't do this!" Billie cried,
hysterically.

"I'm sorry your honor. Billie please, pull yourself
together," Mr. Evans advised.

But Billie was no longer coherent. Everyone's
voices became muted. All she could see was their mouths
moving. The only sound she heard was the sound of her
heart beating loudly from her chest. The room was spinning
at the pace of a roller coaster ride. Billie suddenly became
hot. Sweat poured from her forehead and her throat began
to contract. Her mouth filled with saliva and before she
could excuse herself from the room a stomach full of vomit
spewed from her mouth and onto Mr. Evans lap.

Kyrese was in the hospital for almost three weeks
before he was given the okay from the doctors to go home.
Billie was overjoyed that her baby had made a full
recovery. There were still cuts and scrapes all over his body
but that too would heal with time. Now it was just a matter

of getting him home and comfortable. It was weird entering her home. An eerie quietness filled the sprawling estate. There was no pitter patter of little feet running through the house. Normally, the girls would come charging to the door when she came home but that was all just a memory now.

"Are you happy to be home?" Billie asked Kyrese as they walked through the front door.

"Yes." Kyrese nodded his head.

Knox held him securely by the arm as he walked.

"Where is Kaylee and Kenzie?" Kyrese wondered out loud.

Knox looked at Billie unsure of what to say.

"They're with your father," Billie said, nervously as she and Knox eyed one another.

"Why are they at dad's house? Today isn't Friday." Kyrese continued, confused.

"Because we wanted to make sure you had peace and quiet on your first day back home," Billie lied.

"Oh," Kyrese spoke solemnly.

He'd never admit it to anyone but the whole time he was in the hospital he missed his sisters terribly. They normally drove him crazy but he'd grown accustomed to their pesky behavior. Life wouldn't be normal without it. Once they made it up the winding staircase up to Kyrese's room, Billie pulled back the covers on his bed and helped him inside. It was such a huge relief to have her only son home. She needed the love her children most now.

"Are you hungry? Do you need any of your pain medication right now?" Billie sat on the edge of the bed next to Kyrese.

"I'm a little hungry," Kyrese yawned.

"I'll fix you a nice sandwich and a bowl of potato soup. Does that sound good?" Billie smiled, cheerfully, praying her smile would make Kyrese smile too.

But it didn't. Kyrese was still somber. Billie glanced over her shoulder back at Knox. He stood in the doorway looking on at them. She needed some sort of support from him but like her, Knox was unsure of how to handle Kyrese at such a delicate time.

"When are Kenzie and Kaylee coming home?" Kyrese looked at his mother. "And why didn't dad bring me home with you? Doesn't he miss me? I haven't seen him in over a week."

And there it was. The question that had been hanging over their heads had finally been asked. Billie took a gigantic deep breath. For days she'd been avoiding having this conversation with Kyrese. It had been too painful for her to accept on her own. She still hadn't come to terms that the girls were now living with Cain on a permanent basis.

She'd cried herself to sleep over it every night. Not having her girls at home with her each and every day was like being sent to the electric chair over and over again. But until her appeal hearing in court she'd have to get use to seeing them every other weekend.

"Umm…" Billie cleared her throat. "Your sisters aren't coming home until next weekend." Billie's eyes started to water.

"Why? Is it because of me?" Kyrese questioned worried.

"No, of course not, dear!" Billie lie next to him and held him gently in her arms.

"Then why will they be gone for so long?" Kyrese probed.

"Your sisters will be staying with daddy now majority of the time and will come home to see us every other weekend."

"C'mon ma, just tell me what's going on?" Kyrese said, becoming frustrated. "I know something is wrong. Why am I here and the twins are at daddy's house?"

"Because…" Billie glanced over at Knox.

Just a few weeks ago he would've came to her aid but now he just sat back and watched as she sank. There was no more saving her.

"While you were in the hospital your dad took me to court to gain full custody of your sisters."

"Why just Kenzie and Kaylee? What about me?" Kyrese looked back and forth between Billie and Knox.

Billie could feel herself becoming sick to her stomach but she was determined to remain strong. The words had to be said. Kyrese had to know the truth. There would be no more lies.

"The reason why you're here with me and your sisters are with your dad is because while you were in the hospital a lot of things were revealed."

"What things?"

"Remember before the accident, you asked me if State was your dad?" Billie looked down at him.

"Yes." Kyrese held his breath.

"Well ... he is."

Kyrese lie still and let the words sink in before reacting. He had an inkling that State was really his father but he never thought his hunch would be true.

"So dad isn't my dad, State is?" Kyrese stared at his mother, searching for answers.

"Right, your father." Billie caught herself. "I mean Cain knows this and has decided that he would rather just be your sisters father so you and your real dad can build a relationship."

Billie tried to make the truth sound better.

"So basically, you're telling me that dad doesn't want me anymore." Kyrese's voice trailed off.

"Your dad will always love you, Kyrese." Billie took his face in her hands and gazed deep into his eyes.

"Things are just a lil' different now. Prayerfully you and State will get to know each other and everything will workout fine." Billie tried to convince Kyrese and herself.

"It's not going to be fine mom," Kyrese said, becoming upset. "My father doesn't love me anymore and it's because of you! If you wouldn't have lied none of this would be happening, right now!" Kyrese cried.

"I know honey. It's all my fault and I'm so sorry. I never wanted to hurt you."

"I want my dad! Can you please call my dad!" Kyrese begged.

"I can't sweetie." Billie cried along with him.

"I want to talk to my dad! Knox will you call my dad please!" Kyrese looked at him with tear filled eyes.

"I wish I could buddy." Knox could barely get the words out his heart hurt so bad for Kyrese.

"Noooooo, I want my dad!" Kyrese wailed like a baby.

"I know you do." Billie rocked him in her arms for the next few hours until Kyrese cried his self to sleep.

Are we even gonna make it?
-Beyoncé feat Drake, "Mine"

Chapter 14

By the time Billie was able to leave Kyrese's room her shirt was soaked with tears. She felt like she'd been on the battlefield of war and lost. She thought that finally admitting that she'd lied about Cain being Kyrese's father was hard but telling Kyrese the news was by far the worst moment of her life. As a mother Billie had vowed to keep her children away from harm. She'd vowed to never intentionally hurt them and here she'd done both.

She wasn't sure what to expect from Kyrese from that day moving forward. Learning that Cain wasn't his dad seemed to have killed something inside of him. Billie prayed that she'd be able to fix the broken pieces she'd shattered. After what seemed like a three hour bath, Billie lathered lotion all over her body, placed on a fresh pair of pajamas and climbed into bed. She wasn't going to go to bed until she called the girls and told them goodnight. Five rings later, Cain picked up the phone.

"Yeah," he answered, dryly.

"I just wanted to let you know that I told Kyrese the truth tonight." She shot into the phone. "I hope you're happy."

"You act like you're doing me a favor," Cain scoffed. "He deserved to know the truth."

"He was devastated, Cain. He kept begging me to call you."

"That's on you," Cain replied.

"How can you be so cold hearted? He's your son Cain. No stupid paternity test will change that. Kyrese loves you. You're the only father he knows. How can you disown him like that? He needs you now more than ever."

"You can save the sob story for Maury." Cain yawned in her ear. "Kyrese is yours and City Streets problem now. Ya'll gotta deal with the fall out of this mess, not me. All I'm worried about is Kenzie and Kaylee. Hell, while I'm talking, I sure as hell hope they're mine."

"The twins are your daughters! They look just like you!" Billie shouted, flabbergasted.

"Exactly, and that's the only thing saving yo' ass from me getting a paternity test done on them too."

"Whatever Cain." Billie rolled her eyes. "Can you put the girls on the phone?"

"Gladly," Cain spat. "Kaylee! Your mother is on the phone!"

Seconds later Kaylee picked up the phone.

"What it do mama?" Kaylee asked, out of breath from running.

"Hi, baby girl. How are you today? How was school?" Billie tried to play it cool.

"It was a'ight." Kaylee popped her lips.

"Mama Boots forgot to make our lunch so I had to ask my friend Caitlyn for some lunch money for me and Kenzie but other than that it was straight."

"Oh my god." Billie held her forehead. "I knew that dumb blonde wasn't going to be able to handle this."

"Yeah, homegirl been working my nerves, ma. I mean everyday it's *hi, how you doing, you wanna go outside and play, ya'll hungry?* I just can't," Kaylee sighed.

"I know baby but it will only be for a while. Mama's gonna get you and your sister back in a matter of no time," Billie assured.

"I'm ready to come home now. I hate it here!" Kaylee shouted so her father could here. "I wanna go home!"

"You are home!" Cain shouted back.

"Lies you tell! The devil is a liar!" Kaylee snapped. "I wanna go home wit' my mama! Ya'll ain't even got Nick Jr. over here! What kind of mess is that?!"

"Kaylee watch your mouth," Billie warned. "That is your father you're talking to."

"Well, with your track record that's debatable," Kaylee scoffed.

"You know what? Get yo' ass off this damn phone," Billie barked. "Put Kenzie on the phone!"

"You mad or nah?" Kaylee chuckled, handing her sister the phone.

"What it do Mama Billie?" Kenzie said, playfully.

"Hey mama's baby," Billie spoke sweetly.

"Mama Billie," Kenzie said.

"Yes, Kenzie."

"Is Kyrese still sleeping with the fishes?"

"No!" Billie giggled. "Your brother is alive and well. You will see him next weekend when you come home."

"That's what up. Mama Billie—"

"Kenzie?" Billie stopped her.

"Ma'am?"

"Why do you and your sister keep calling me Mama Billie?"

"Cause Mama Boots said we need to call you Mama Billie and her Mama."

"What?!" Billie screeched. "That heffa said what?"

"Mmm hmm, she sure did chile." Kenzie clicked her tongue. "She said that since she's our new full time mommy we need to start calling her Mama. But me and Kaylee weren't down with that so we compromised and said we'd call her Mama Boots."

"I'ma kill her," Billie fumed.

"Calm down. You ain't gotta go all Mama Pope on her. We good. By the time we through wit' Mama Boots she gon' be wishing we were back at home with you."

"Just don't poison her, beat her or burn down the house," Billie laughed.

"Huuuuuh okay." Kenzie giggled along with her mother.

"I love you. Be a good girl for mommy and I'll talk to you tomorrow."

"Love you too Mama Billie. I mean mommy." Kenzie corrected herself.

"Bye Kenzie." Billie ended the call.

She wished like hell that she was the one putting her girls to bed. That day would prayerfully come soon. Billie situated herself underneath the covers and watched adoringly as Knox exited his private master bathroom. It had been weeks since she'd paid attention to his handsome face and succulent body. Both were on full display. All he wore after his shower was a white cotton towel wrapped securely around his waist. His pecks were nice and firm.

The six pack of muscles in his stomach rippled down his pelvis. Everything about Knox was enticing. He was the first white man that she'd ever been physically attracted to. She missed the intimacy they use to share. She missed how they use to long for one another. All of that seemed like a distant memory now. Even when they were in the same room it felt like they were ocean apart. Billie wanted that old thing back but because of her deceit it appeared that this would be their fate.

"You talk to the girls?" Knox removed his towel and slipped on a pair of plaid pajama bottoms.

The sight of his long, thick dick dangling inside his pants sent chills throughout Billie's body. It had been ages since she felt the pulsating, rhythm of his instrument inside of her warm, wet walls. She needed her husband. She wanted him but the question remained did he feel the same way?

"Yeah, apparently Puss-n-Boots has them calling her Mama now."

"Wow." Knox shook his head. "The crazy train just doesn't stop, does it?" He chuckled.

"But you know Kenzie and Kaylee bad asses wasn't having it so they're calling her Mama Boots," Billie snickered. "This appeal hearing can't come fast enough. I can't have my babies over there with them idiots on a full time basis. Their stupidity might rub off on them."

"We don't want that to happen." Knox, replied, applying lotion to his chest and arms.

"You need any help?" Billie asked, trying to maintain her composure.

"Naw, I'm good." Knox put the lotion up.

"Oh… okay," Billie responded, sadly.

"I'm tired as fuck," Knox yawned, stretching his arms. "Today has been a long ass day."

"Yes, it has." Billie pulled back the covers for him.

Knox walked around the bed to his side. Billie naturally assumed that he was about to get into bed with her. Instead Knox grabbed his pillow and pulled the covers back up.

"Where are you going?" Billie asked, confused.

"In the guest room." Knox tucked the pillow under his arm.

"Why?"

185

"C'mon Billie we gotta stop pretending like shit between us is good. I'ma keep it one hundred wit' you. I don't' really vibe wit' you like that no more. And to be all the way honest, I don't trust you. I just look at it like if you can keep such a huge secret like that from me, what else can you be hiding?"

"I'm not hiding anything else, though." Billie explained as she felt him inch further and further away from her.

"Yeah, that's what your mouth say but we both know your word ain't shit," Knox stated, bluntly.

"That's a bit much, Knox." Billie willed herself not cry.

"It hurts doesn't it?" He ignored her tears.

"Is that your intention, to hurt me? Cause if so, you're succeeding." Billie blinked away the tears.

"No it's not actually. I'm just trying to make sense of all of this. You and I were already struggling. This shit just made it ten times worse. I just need a minute to process all of this so I'ma take my ass in the other room and go to bed." Knox walked towards her.

"Goodnight." He kissed her gently on the forehead.

"Goodnight." Billie whispered as he turned his back to leave.

She wanted to shout after him to not leave, that she loved him and that she was sorry but the look in his eyes proved that no words would change his mind about her. Their marriage was doomed and Billie wasn't sure if there was anyway to fix it.

The holiday season was in full swing. It was the end of September and Edible Couture was filled with customers gathering up sinful treats for Halloween. Dylan loved this time of year. Not only was it the busiest time of the year at her bakery but she loved any excuse to shop. She'd already bought Mason several Halloween costumes, numerous decorations for the house and more candy than any woman, man or child could consume. She was also super excited about expanding her business.

With the success of her show on the Food Network, her New York Times Best-Selling dessert book, business was at an all time high. It was now time for Dylan to open another Edible Couture. This time she was going to open a bakery in New York. Dylan was over the moon about her expansion plans. It was a huge undertaking with being a wife, raising Mason, doing the show, running the first

Edible Couture and writing another dessert book but it was all worth it.

She'd finally found her calling. Dylan still had a lot to prove to herself and to the world. While the bakery buzzed with customers buying scrumptious treats Dylan, her manager and her team of contractors sat in the back of the bakery discussing the new location's floor plan. Life was great for Dylan. She and Angel were on good terms. His fight was soon approaching and he was in the best shape of his life. They were making plans to build their dream home. Mason was growing by the day. Her business was thriving and Kyrese was home and doing well.

She missed Billie terribly but the anger and pain from her betrayal kept Dylan at bay. She didn't have time for drama in her life. After what Billie had done, Dylan couldn't trust her again. There was no way their friendship could be mended. Dylan was determined to move forward with her life without Billie. But drama was always lurking around Dylan. It was never too far away. As she and her contractors were wrapping up their meeting, State came walking into the bakery.

Dylan looked up at him and immediately the smile that was on her face vanished. Just as much as she despised Billie she hated State even more. After years of being in a relationship with him where he treated her like crap, she'd found space in her heart for forgiveness. Never did she imagine that the things he'd put her through in the past could be trumped. She'd thought he'd done it all to her. He and Billie were slick to keep such a huge secret from her. It was as if they enjoyed making a fool out of her.

"Excuse me." Dylan smiled to the group of men as she rose from her seat. "I have an unexpected guest."

Dylan walked gracefully over to State with a warm smile on her face. Through a clenched jaw, she spoke in a low tone and said, "Outside now."

State followed Dylan out doors. Dylan walked a few doors down from her bakery then spun around on her heels.

"Let's get this straight. You and I are done. I have nothing else in life to say to you. You disgust me."

"I know you're upset but just let me explain how everything went down," State reasoned.

"Nigga you are twelve years too late for a fuckin' explanation. You can save it. I don't wanna hear that shit." Dylan put her hand up in his face to shut him up.

"By the time I found out that Billie was your homegirl, I had already caught feelings for you." State still tried to explain.

"If you cared for me so much then you should've told me the truth when you found out. I've known you for almost six years now and I'm just not finding out the truth. That to me is some bullshit."

"You're right. I completely agree. I should've told you and for that I'm sorry," State sincerely apologized.

"Nigga fuck you and your lousy ass, I'm sorry!" Dylan spat sarcastically. "Don't reach out to me and don't ever come to my place of business again." She shot storming off.

"Dylan! On some real shit, I'm sorry!" State yelled after her.

Instead of answering verbally, Dylan hit him with the middle finger and switched her way back into the bakery.

**Underneath the pretty face is something complicated.
-Beyoncé, "No Angel"**

Chapter 15

After another week of resting and gathering his strength, it was time for Kyrese to return to school. Billie was ecstatic that her baby was back to his normal self. She no longer had to help him around the house. His bruises were almost healed and he seemed to be coping with the news of State being his father somewhat well. State called him everyday but Billie wasn't ready for them to start having in-home visits yet. She honestly didn't think Kyrese was ready for it either.

She couldn't quite read where he was at, mentally. Kyrese was always recluse when it came to his feelings. He never liked talking about his thoughts, hopes, dreams or fears. Billie tried her best to get information out of him but no amount of ass kissing or sweet talk worked. Dressed in her silk robe, she walked sleepily down the hall to Kyrese's room to wake him for school. On her way to his room she stopped by Knox room to see if he was still asleep. It was so weird to have her husband sleeping in the guest room.

Billie crept towards the door and poked her head inside only to find the bed still made up from the day before. Completely thrown off by his absence, she stepped inside the bedroom and looked around. There was no sign of Knox anywhere.

"Knox!" She called out to get no answer.

So this muthafucka didn't come home last night, she thought as her heart raced. She couldn't fathom that Knox would disrespect her by not coming home. Sure they were experiencing a rough patch but had things really gotten that bad? Billie swallowed the hurt she was feeling and bottled it up for later. She had to concentrate on her son. He was the most important issue in her life. Gathering her emotions she left the room and tried to forget that her husband was somewhere else than home.

"Kyrese," Billie said, softly knocking on his door. "It's time to get up, baby."

She unlocked the door and walked in. To her surprise, Kyrese was already up and getting dressed.

"Well, look who's up and ready," she smiled.

"I couldn't sleep." Kyrese slipped on a pair of crisp white socks.

"You weren't hurting or anything, were you?" Billie asked, grabbing his shoes for him.

"No, I just had a lot on my mind." Kyrese put on his right shoe.

"Oh." Billie stood quietly.

She knew exactly what plagued his mind. It was all the drama she'd caused.

"I'm sorry."

"Mom ... you don't have to keep saying you're sorry. It is what it is. I don't care." Kyrese, snapped with an attitude.

The mother in Billie wanted to check him for snapping at her but the guilt she carried day in and day out wouldn't allow it.

"You want French toast and fruit for breakfast?" She asked, changing the subject.

"I don't care." Kyrese put his books inside his book bag.

Billie wanted to reach out and hug her son 'cause she knew that he needed all of the love the world had to offer but Kyrese wouldn't let her in. Every time she tried to talk to him he was cold. Everyone in her life was shutting her out. She never felt more alone. Every night she cried herself to sleep. She needed the love of her family. Billie pulled her self together and pretended as if she was okay. The bruise on her heart said otherwise though as she headed to the kitchen.

It only took her a half hour to make breakfast. It felt weird to only be cooking for two instead five. On a normal Monday morning the kitchen would be filled with children, laughter and the sound of forks scrapping plates. Kyrese came into the kitchen dressed in his school uniform ready for school.

"You want orange or apple juice?" Billie smiled, placing his plate down on the kitchen island.

"A bottle of water please." Kyrese stood instead of sitting down.

"You can sit down and eat." Billie handed him the bottle water.

"I'm not hungry." Kyrese said, stoned face. "I'ma just head to the bus stop." He turned around to leave.

"Hold up!" Billie quickly ran after him. "You need to eat something before you go, Kyrese!"

"I'll grab something at school, ma."

"You have a whole breakfast in the kitchen you can eat," Billie rebutted.

"I don't want that anymore," Kyrese replied, thoroughly annoyed.

Beyond ready to get away from his mother he unlocked the front door and stepped outside. Billie knew he was testing her. She was trying her damnedest not to explode but he was really taking her there. Right when she was about to go off she saw State get out of his car. Shocked to see him, Billie swiftly closed her robe so he wouldn't see her silk negligee underneath.

It didn't matter if Billie closed her robe or not. State could still see her hardened nipples poke through the fabric. Whenever she was in State's presence Billie was overcome with lust. His height and sexy chocolate skin turned her on to the fullest and when he spoke time stood still. It wasn't even 8:00a.m and he looked like he'd stepped clean out of GQ magazine.

Like always State's hair was freshly cut. He rocked a low cut like no other. His salt and pepper goatee and pearly white teeth complimented the white and black striped cashmere sweater, gold Rolex watch, black fitted jeans and Giuseppe Zanotti sneakers well. Billie couldn't figure out how she would survive a lifetime of raising their son together without bending over and letting him have his way with her.

"What are you doing here?" She furrowed her brows.

"I came to see Kyrese off to school. It is your first day back, right?" State asked Kyrese.

"Yes." Kyrese responded, surprised to see his father as well.

"Here, I brought you a caramel macchiato." State handed Kyrese the drink.

"He's twelve State. He doesn't drink that kind of stuff," Billie mocked.

"Thanks State." Kyrese defied his mother and took a sip.

Billie's nostrils flared like a bull, she was so mad.

"Your bus is going to get here in a minute, ain't it?" State asked, Kyrese.

"Yeah."

"Is it alright if I walk with you?"

"I guess," Kyrese shrugged.

"Umm hello?" Billie waved her hands in the air. "Have you asked me how I feel about you walking him to the bus stop?"

"No," State screwed up his face. "I don't have to and instead of worrying about me you need to fall back and go put some clothes on."

Kyrese hung his head and snickered.

"Really?" Billie scoffed, appalled.

"Really," State mocked her. "You out here looking quite THOTish." He and Kyrese laughed as Knox pulled up the driveway.

All eyes went to him. Knox put the car in park and got out.

"Morning everybody." he spoke.

"I thought you were in the house sleep," Kyrese said.

"Nah, man." Knox stared at Billie.

He could see the anger and hurt in her eyes. He wasn't trying to hurt her on purpose but Knox had to put his feelings first this time.

"I see you found your way home," Billie spat.

"Good morning to you too Billie." Knox bypassed her and went inside.

Billie stood frozen in time. She wanted desperately to lash out at him for disrespecting her and their marriage but she had to remember that she was the one who brought them to this dark place.

"Trouble in paradise?" State arched his brow.

"Mind your business, please," Billie grimaced.

A few minutes later Kyrese's bus pulled up. State and Billie both told him goodbye and to have a good day. Both parents watched in silence as his bus pulled off down the street. Once it was out of eye sight, Billie turned to State and said, "I understand that you're Kyrese's father but you can't just be popping up all willy nilly when you want to. We have to have some kind of order."

"It cracks me up that after all of these years; you still haven't learned to loosen up. I mean you already out her on the bus stop in full THOT wear," State joked.

"Does it look like I'm laughing?" Billie replied, with a straight face.

"A'ight you're right. I should've called first but I knew if I did you were going to say no."

"You damn right I would've said no," Billie agreed. "I don't even know how I feel about all of this yet."

"What you mean?"

"I can't risk you doing to Kyrese, what you did to me. My baby has gone through enough and I am going to shield him from any and all pain that I can prevent."

"What I did to you was fucked up but I wouldn't intentionally hurt Kyrese. He's my s…" State choked on his words. "He's my so…"

"Look at you! You can't even say the word," Billie screeched.

"Son! He's my son!" State shouted. "Kyrese… What's his middle name?" He asked, Billie.

"Demetrius." Billie rolled her eyes to the sky.

"Kyrese Demetrius Adanu is my son! I have a freakin' son!" State shouted to the heavens. "How cool is that?"

"First of all his last name is Townsend and second of all stop all that goddamn shouting! I have neighbors," Billie shrieked, stomping off.

"Umm Kyrese will be taking my last." State shot catching up with her.

"Over my dead body."

"Well you better get to dying then," State quipped. "What is your problem? You mad 'cause your dude ain't come home last night?"

"I swear to god you are nosey as fuck. Do you know how to mind your own business?"

"Not really," State grinned.

"Please do us both a favor and stay out of mine."

"I gotta admit though." State glanced back at her ass that bounced with every step she took. "You lookin' kind of right in that robe."

Billie stopped in her tracks and folded her arms across her chest.

"Like seriously, what is wrong with you? Do you get off on tormenting me?" She questioned about to flip.

200

"A little bit," State chuckled. "You're so cute when you're mad."

"I don't have time for your shit right now," Billie said, sternly.

State noticed the anxiety that was building by the minute inside of her. She couldn't even look at him directly in his eyes. She was on the verge of tears. Billie wasn't the type of broad who cried. She was way too prideful for that but the tears were sitting right at the brim of her eyes begging to fall.

"My bad. I wasn't trying to upset you. I was honestly trying to make you laugh," State said, sincerely.

"As you can see I'm in no mood to laugh. I just want my fuckin' life back!" Billie's voice rose. "I gotta go." She walked up her driveway.

"A'ight." State replied, feeling genuinely bad for her. "I'll be back when Kyrese gets out of school!"

"Whatever!" Billie waved her hand, not in the mood to fight.

With the weight of the world on her shoulders, she walked inside of the house in search of Knox. Homeboy had some serious explaining to do. Billie found him in their bedroom packing one of the Louis Vuitton suitcases she'd bought for him. Alarmed by the sight she stopped dead in her tracks.

"You taking an unexpected trip," she asked.

"Nah," Knox placed a stack of shirts inside the suitcase. "I've been thinking it's best for the both of us if I move out."

"So you go from sleeping in the guest room, to not coming home at night to moving out?" Billie shot in disbelief.

Knox didn't know how to respond without hurting her feelings even more so he chose to stay quiet.

"Look." Billie took him by the arm and made him look at her. "I know that what I did was wrong but we can work this out. Can you at least give me the chance to earn your trust back?"

"It's not even just about trust. You don't respect me as a man. You never have," Knox admitted. "I've never felt equal to you in this marriage. It's your way or no way."

"That's not true." Billie retorted, feeling him slipping away from her.

"Billie, you talk to me like I'm one of your kids. I'm a grown ass muthafuckin' man. You lying about the paternity of Kyrese was just the icing on the cake. I can't take it anymore. You're frigid, you're mean and you're

202

way too bougie. I mean damn, the only time you smile is when you want something. You won't even give me no head," Knox exploded.

"I'm sick of it, man! I want to be happy. I'm tired of pretending that I am. I want the real thing and you can't give me that 'cause you're not happy with yourself."

That was all Billie could take. She'd been shot point blank in the heart. Knox had killed her. It would take the strength of god to bring her back to life. Her mind told her to speak, to fight for her marriage but his confession had silenced her. Everything he's said about her was true. There was no denying or sugar-coating it.

She'd treated him more like an assistant that she fucked every now and then than a husband. She didn't treat him like her equal. Knox did deserve more; more than she had to offer him. It still however hurt like hell to see him go. She'd loved him. She'd thought or at least tried to pretend that he was the one.

She thought that with him she would be different. She wouldn't push him away like she'd done Cain but she had. Now here she was alone, yet again picking up the pieces of shattered dreams that lie scattered around her feet. She'd run him away like she'd done everyone else in her life. Billie wanted to let go. She wished that she could love freely but after the hurt State had caused she'd conditioned herself to close off any and all emotion. Billie would only give so much of herself before she closed herself off. The only people in the world she gave every crevice of herself to were her kids.

She was so shell-shocked with the news that Knox was leaving her that she hadn't even noticed that he'd kissed her on the cheek and left. Before she realized it, the entire day had gone by and she was lying on the couch in the living room, staring at the ceiling. She hadn't bathed. Alex Isley played softly as she drowned in the million of tears that fell from her eyes. This was her rock bottom.

Everything that she loved was gone. She'd lost it all, her girls, her best friend and now her husband. Billie wanted nothing more than to sink into an abyss and disappear. She couldn't withstand the hurt she endured another day. She was so lost in her tears and sorrow that she didn't remember to lock the front door. After ringing the doorbell several times, State took it upon his self to walk inside the house.

"Hello?" He called out but got no answer.

He could hear music playing in the distance so he followed the sound. State surprisingly found Billie sprawled out on the couch in a heap of tears.

"Damn, what's wrong with you?" He eyed her concerned.

"What the hell are you doing in my house?" Billie groaned, closing her eyes.

"I rang the doorbell, I don't how many times. I told you I was coming back."

"Kyrese isn't here yet so you can leave." She rolled over so her back could face him.

"He will be in a minute." State looked around in awe. "Yo' I don't know what's going on with you but he doesn't need to see you like this."

"Like what?"

"Have you looked at yourself in a mirror? Your hair is all over your head and your eyes are swollen and blood shot red. What happened after I left this morning? You and ole boy got into it or something?" State's London accent echoed throughout the room.

"Didn't I tell you to mind your fuckin' business?" Billie replied in a sarcastic tone.

"You're the mother of my son. You're business is my business if it's going to affect our son," State checked her.

"Mom! I'm home!" Kyrese shouted, coming through the door.

"Oh god," Billie groaned, holding her head. "I can't let him see me like this." She buried her face underneath a throw pillow.

"I told your hard head ass that," State remarked. "I got him, man."

State met Kyrese in the foyer. Every time he laid eyes on Kyrese he was amazed at how much they looked a like. Kyrese had his coco skin, almond shaped eyes, body build and even the same mole under his eye.

"What up, lil' dude?" He extended his hand for a five.

"Hi." Kyrese looked at him like he was an idiot.

"No high-five? Okay, I can live with that." State put his hand down.

"Where's my mom?" Kyrese took off his book bag.

"She's taking a nap. She's not feeling good today."

"Ok but what are you doing here?" Kyrese asked, curiously.

"I came by to spend some time with you."

"Oh ..." Kyrese responded, smelling something fishy. "Let me go check on my mom." He tried to bypass State.

"Hold up a minute." State stopped him. "She's sleep. How about me and you go upstairs to your room and start on homework while your mom gets some rest."

"I'm good. I can do my homework by myself." Kyrese stared at him quizzically.

He knew something was up but didn't want to press the issue.

"You might be good but I'ma help you anyway." State followed Kyrese up the steps to his room.

It took State and Kyrese a little over an hour to finish all of his homework. Kyrese barely made eye contact or talked to him. He knew that State was his father but he didn't know him from a can of paint. He idolized him as a celebrity but as his dad there was no connection. Kyrese wanted the man he'd known as his father his entire life to be helping him with his homework. He needed Cain to tell him that he loved him and that he was still his son no matter what.

He didn't want to build a relationship with State. He wanted his old family back. Kyrese hated feeling like an outsider. He always felt a disconnection with Cain but he was still his dad. Kyrese figured one day he'd do something that would make him proud and he'd love him like he loved Kenzie and Kaylee. Now it seemed that day would never come. Everyday that Kyrese awoke to the misery that existed in his life he wanted to run away.

He was only twelve. He couldn't process his feelings or his new reality like the adults could. He appreciated that his mother tried to ease his pain but she was the cause of it all. He despised her. She used to be his savior now she was his mortal enemy. Kyrese didn't care that she was young when she'd made the decision to lie. Her foolish decision had ruined his life. He couldn't and wouldn't forgive her for it.

For the rest of the evening, State did everything in his power to keep Kyrese occupied while Billie lay on the couch in mourning. State was new to this whole parenting thing so talking to Kyrese and trying to connect with him was difficult. State tried to talk about sports with him but Kyrese basically ignored him. Talking to him about music was a bust. Kyrese treated him as if he wasn't even there.

State didn't know what to do. If they had anything in common Kyrese sure wasn't acting like it. Despite his hard exterior, State still looked upon his son with joy and pride. He never imagined his self as a father but now that he was, he felt like his existence on earth really meant something. He was determined to build a relationship with Kyrese. He was his mini me.

Sure, it wouldn't be easy but nothing in life worth having came easy. That night State was on total daddy duty. He made sure that Kyrese finished his homework, bathed, ate dinner and went to bed on time. Once Kyrese was squared away for the night it was time for State to deal with Billie. He was over her pity party. He didn't care about the details. He just wanted her to be okay. She still hadn't moved from the couch.

"Billie!" He nudged her arm.

"What?" She responded with an attitude.

"It's time for you to get up."

"Thank you for helping me with Kyrese tonight but you can go now, I'm fine."

"I'm not going no where until you get your ass up!" State pulled her over onto her back.

"Please leave me alone," Billie whined.

"Oh you think it's a game." State lifted her up into his strong arms.

"If you don't' put me down!" Billie kicked and screamed.

She tried slapping him in the face but missed.

"I'm trying to help yo' dumb ass," State barked.

"I don't need your help!" Billie sank her teeth into his shoulder.

"Bitch are you crazy?!" State winced in pain.

"Obviously, can't you tell?" Billie said with a sudden fierceness.

"Don't bite me no more," State warned. "Calm the fuck down!" He demanded.

Billie honestly didn't have the energy to put up a fight. She just wanted peace and for the thoughts in her mind to cease. All the truthful but venomous words Knox spewed that morning exposed the broken areas in her heart that she'd been trying to conceal for years. She prided herself on being strong and not showing any real emotions. Being totally transparent was like her shield.

She couldn't risk opening herself up to the world 'cause what she'd discovered at a young age was that the world was cruel. She was secretly jealous of how open and free Dylan was. Dylan didn't mind being hurt. No matter what she always picked herself up and tried again. Billie was taught by her mother to be emotionless and to turn a blind eye. All of her life she was controlled by her mother. Billie was thrilled when her mother packed up and moved to France.

She no longer had to worry about what her mother thought or felt. It just sucked that now that her life had blown up in flames she was left to deal with the aftermath alone. State carried Billie's limp, weak body up the staircase and to her room. Once inside the master bathroom, he placed Billie down onto her feet and began to run her a bath. State dimmed the lights and lit the candles that were strategically placed all around the bathroom.

A soft amber glow lit the entire room. State filled the sunken tub with steaming hot water, bubbles and jasmine scented bath beads. Once it was filled he turned the water off and stood in front of Billie. What appeared to be a million of dried up tears graced her face. She was a weak shell of herself. In all the years he'd known her he'd never seen her distraught.

It looked as if she'd reached her breaking point. Although she was a bitch to him State actually felt bad for her. She needed someone to take care of her and he planned on being that somebody. State stood gazing into her tear-filled eyes. Complete silence surrounded them. All you could hear was drips of water falling from the faucet. It had been twelve years since they were this close.

Billie couldn't tell if he pitied her or was sincerely concerned for her well being. Either way she didn't have the strength to figure it out. All she knew was that she needed comfort and State was there to give it to her so she was willing to accept it. State saw the years of pain inside of Billie through the windows of her eyes. For years, he'd done everything in his power to ignore it 'cause he knew he was partially to blame. But that night there was no denying it.

With the light from the candles flickering around them, State gently removed her robe and negligee. They both fell in a heap to the floor. Billie stood before him physically and emotionally naked. Her body was just as flawless as it was when they were in their twenties. Her soft brown breasts saluted him while the curves of her hips begged to be caressed.

State had to remind himself to be a gentleman. He didn't want Billie to think that his kind gesture was just a ploy to fuck. As they stared into each other's eyes, State lifted Billie back up into his arms and placed her gently down into the steaming hot water. The water felt like heaven. It was just what she needed. State sat beside the tube and looked upon her face. All of the old feelings he'd placed on pause for her were starting to replay.

She was his first love. No other woman since her could tame him. Now here they were back in each others life, raising a son. It was them against the world. State picked up her pink bath sponge, placed body wash onto it and began to bathe her. Billie watched silently as he lathered her body with sweet scented soap. No man had ever bathed her but the fact still remained that he was the reason she lie depressed.

He'd been her biggest mistake. All of these years he'd been engraved inside of her memory. No other man had been able to capture her heart the way he had. She thought back then that they'd raise their child and ride into the sunset but her future held a different story. She'd been able to fill her life with other men as a distraction from how she really felt but he was always there. Tears stung her eyes as she looked upon his handsome face.

"What's wrong?" State asked, wiping her tears away with his thumb.

"You ruined me," Billie confessed, crying. "I loved you and you just left me. What the fuck was I suppose to do with that?" She covered her face with her wet hands.

"My life is a mess because of you. I wasn't supposed to end up like this. We were supposed to be together. I thought we were set in stone."

"Billie, I'm sorry," State replied, remorsefully.

"You? I'm sorry. I can't believe that all of these years later that I still care. I've tried so hard to forget you. I even tricked myself into believing that I hated you. I haven't been able to fully give my heart to a man since you and that's mainly because..." Billie paused.

The words she were about to say were like atom bombs. Once she said them there would be no turning back.

"I still love yo' ass. Lord knows I don't want to but I do," she sobbed.

State sat back, stunned. He had no idea that what he'd done had affected her in such a way.

"I should've handled you better back then but I was young and reckless. I loved the fuck outta you and that scared the shit outta me. I wasn't expecting to fall for you the way I did but I knew at the time that I couldn't be what you needed me to be. Instead of telling you that I did what I knew how to do best, which was to not feel," State responded, honestly.

"But I'm not on that shit no more. I'm not out here wilding out no more. I got Kyrese to think of now. I want to be a better man for him."

Billie allowed his words to sink in. She wanted desperately to believe him so she said a silent prayer to god hoping that she could trust State this time. It felt good to know that the love she thought he had for her wasn't imaginary or one sided. The question still remained did he love her now because Billie couldn't pretend like her heart wasn't in the palm of his hand anymore. With him was were her heart lay. She didn't have all of the answers but she knew she wanted him.

"Come on little trouble maker." State helped her stand up. "It's time for us to go bed." He grabbed a towel and dried her body.

For the first time that day Billie smiled. When they were younger he always called her his little trouble maker. Billie's feisty behavior was always a turn on to him. Once she was dry, State wrapped the towel and his arms around her waist. State nestled his nose in the crook her neck and inhaled her scent. She smelled like an erotic garden.

Billie knew she should've been nervous but being in State's arms felt like home. If he kept it up, she could see herself falling for him once more. Billie couldn't make any sense as to where their relationship was heading but things couldn't get any worse than it already was. It was mind-blogging to her however to be back in his arms. She thought that she'd closed the door on a romance with State, yet here she was.

Every part of her wanted to give in and wrap her legs around his waist but the part of her heart that he'd stomped on wouldn't allow it. State softly kissed the nape of her neck then took her hand and led her into the bedroom. Being the gentleman he was he massaged lotion onto her body and helped her slip on a crème silk negligee. Billie lie on her side and watched as State removed his sweater.

Billie watched with lust in her eyes. She couldn't believe this was happening. A few weeks before State was her sworn enemy now he was her only ally. The wife beater he wore underneath his sweater clung to his chest, exposing his toned pecks and abs. State was sexier now then he was when they were twenty-three. Before hopping into bed State blew out the candles in the bathroom. Billie didn't know what was about to happen but she welcomed the adventure.

State slipped into bed and lie behind her. Billie's back was pressed up against his chest. She could feel the thickness of his dick on the cheeks of her ass. She wondered would it be tacky or whorish to reach back and touch it. Once again, Billie had to remind herself that she was a married woman. Her husband however had technically left her. She was free to do as she pleased.

Having State rock her pussy to sleep was all she yearned for.

"Billie," State stressed her name.

"Huh?" She said, breathlessly.

"Go to sleep, baby. We ain't fuckin' tonight." He kissed the back of her head. "You ain't ready for this dick, baby-girl."

Billie tried her damnedest not to laugh but failed miserably. Just like back in the day, State knew her every thought.

He like to call me Peaches when
we get this nasty.
-Beyoncé, "Partition"

Chapter 16

Dylan lay completely naked on her back in front of her new fire place. The heat from the roaring fire warmed her body. The house was pitch black except for the gold flickers of light from the fire. Angel lay on top of her. His face hovered over hers. Fully aroused by her flawless frame, he kissed her lips hungrily. Dylan relished the taste of his tongue.

Angel placed a trail of sweet kisses from Dylan's lips down to her belly button. Dylan looked on eagerly awaiting the moment when his lips met with her clit. Angel knew what she wanted so instead he kissed her thighs and legs. Dylan shrieked in agony. They'd been making love for hours and still hadn't gotten enough of one another. She loved when she and Angel had days like this. Neither of them was willing to back down or give in. They had to have one another.

"Oooh baby suck my pussy," Dylan moaned, going insane.

"That's what you want?" Angel teased her by licking her clit quickly.

"Yes!"

Always one to give his wife exactly what she wanted, Angel gave in and feasted on her kitty.

"Awwwww baby, that feels good." Dylan closed her eyes tight. "Aww yeah," she moaned as Angel licked circles around her hard clit.

"Awww yeah, lick my pussy." Dylan opened her eyes and watched with delight in her eyes.

Angel was flicking his tongue across Dylan's throbbing clit at lightening speed. He'd buried his entire face in her pussy. Dylan enjoyed every second of it.

"Fuck that feels so good!"

"You like that shit, don't you?" Angel spit on her pussy and massaged the juices into her skin.

"You know I do," Dylan moaned, sitting up.

She had to taste him. Angel got on his knees. His long, thick, dick dangled in front of Dylan's face. Her mouth watered like a starving child. She couldn't help but devour his entire dick while playing with her pussy.

"That's right, play with that pussy, baby." Angel caressed her breasts.

There was nothing sexier to him than to watch his wife play with herself right in from him. The visual made his dick rock hard. Dylan did as she was told and rotated her fingers clockwise across her clit. The feeling of sucking her husband's dick while masturbating was mind-blowing. Angel grabbed the back of Dylan's head and made her look at him.

"You love me?"

"Yes," she whimpered, feeling herself about to cum.

Angel leaned down and kissed her with so much intensity that Dylan had no choice but to climax. Wet sticky cream was all over hand. Dylan massaged her juices onto Angel's dick as she stroked his penis. Angel couldn't take it anymore. He had to be inside of her. On his back he pulled Dylan on top of him. In a matter of seconds his dick was inside of her warm walls. Angel gripped her ass and pumped his long rod in and out of her at a feverish pace.

"Oooh yeah, daddy! Fuck me!" Dylan screamed. "Oooooh yeah, baby! Ahhhhhhhh! Shit Angel, fuck me with that big cock! Mmmmm that feels so good! Awww yeah! Aww baby! I wanna see you cum!"

"You wanna see it?" Angel groaned.

"Yeah!" Dylan bounced up and down on his dick.

She could feel Angel about to explode. With each thrust they both neared climaxing.

"Fuck! I'm about to cum!" Angel slapped her ass cheek.

"Me too, baby!" Dylan screeched cumming all over his dick.

Angel released hot cum into her sugar walls. For a while they both lay in silence collecting their strength.

"Shit nigga," Dylan moaned, lying on top of his chest. "That I ain't going to jail dick something else," she teased.

"I told you it's not a game." Angel leaned over to take a swig of Paul Mason.

"I'm just so happy that we were able to settle everything out of court. I would've lost my goddamn mind if you had to go jail."

"Shit you … me too but I told you everything was going to be fine. That nigga just wanted a come up so I threw a couple of stacks at him and he flew his dumbass back over to Australia or wherever the fuck he from."

"He's from France," Dylan laughed.

"I don't give a fuck where that nigga from. What did you see in that lame ass dude anyway? He wack as fuck." Angel mean mugged her.

"I was having a temporary lapse of memory." Dylan rolled her eyes.

"You mean temporary lapse of judgment." Angel corrected her.

"Whatever." Dylan waved him off. "The shit is behind us now. We have our new house." She gushed, looking around the sprawling estate.

Their new home was well over 10,000 square feet and located in the Central West End section of St. Louis. The Venetian-Italianate architecture mansion had stained glass windows and a carriage house with two apartments. There were eight bedrooms and five bathrooms. Majority of the mansion had hardwood floors but on the second level the entire floor was made of marble. Off the dining room was a covered porch. The kitchen counters were made of Italian marble and Dylan's favorite feature of the mansion were the pocket doors.

"Now we can concentrate on your next match, me opening up the next Edible Couture location in New York and most importantly expanding our family," Dylan twirled her index finger around on Angel's chest.

"I want Mason to have a little sister so bad and they'll only be two years apart if I get pregnant soon which will be great."

"The way I just fucked you, you're probably pregnant with quadruplets," Angel grinned.

"You did hit me wit' the death stroke," Dylan sat up.

Her full, perky breasts were all Angel could concentrate on.

"I'm so happy that you're my wife." He cupped her breasts in his hands and pulled her down so he could devour them.

Angel's wet tongue danced circles around Dylan's harden nipples.

"You trying to go for round four?" Dylan moaned, licking her upper lip.

"I'm trained to go twelve. You down?" Angel asked, inserting his dick into her eager slit.

"You ain't said nothing but a word," Dylan rotated her hips clockwise.

The sound of six inch Louboutin stiletto heels clicked against Dylan's marble floor. She was giving Tee-Tee a tour of her new home.

"Bitch!" Tee-Tee turned and looked at her in awe. "Ya'll did the muthafuckin' thing. Girl, this place is breathtaking. You sure ya'll ain't put out a sex tape to get this 'cause I heard Mimi and Niko are down in Atlanta doing it," Tee-Tee snapped his finger.

"Trust me if I put out a sex tape, you'd know about it. Mimi and Niko sex life ain't got shit on me and Angel's. We gets down," Dylan stated, bluntly.

"How many rooms ya'll got? Me, Bernard and Princess Gaga might be moving in."

"You silly," Dylan laughed.

"You laughing but bitch I'm serious," Tee-Tee smirked. "I be forgetting Angel net worth. Homeboy is doing it big and doing it well."

"Umm excuse you." Dylan cocked her head back. "I put in on this too."

"I'm sure you did." Tee-Tee patted her on the arm sympathetically. "I'm sure you sprinkled a few coins in but let's keep it all the way one hundred. This house smells of *mill-ions*. This mansion has to be well over ten million dollars. Now am I wrong or am I right?" He arched his eyebrow.

"You're right!" Dylan burst out laughing. "My nigga is the shit!" She high-fived her cousin.

"Where is our boo at anyway?" Tee-Tee referred to Angel.

"At the gym."

"Girl, this house is so big I can't even hear my baby."

"Princess and Mason are straight. My nanny Jaime has them and I have video monitors in each room," Dylan assured.

"Bitch you know yo' ass is in another tax bracket. That's some rich folks shit."

"Shut up," Dylan playfully pushed him.

"So." Tee-Tee popped his lips as they entered Dylan's in home movie theater. "You gon' invite Billie over to see the new crib?"

"Uh … no, " Dylan cocked her head back, appalled. "The kids of course will be over but she can stay her ass where she at."

"Listen," Tee-Tee sat down in one of the theater seats. "What she did was fucked up on so many levels but ya'll are sisters. She loves you and you love her. It's not like you're not going to be around each other. You're married to the girl's brother and she's still my friend."

"And you're telling me this because?" Dylan said, clearly agitated.

"I'm telling you this because life is too short to be holding onto grudges. She's apologized. She can't rewind time and make it all go away. You have to find a way in your heart to forgive her."

"Let her fuck Bernard and have a child by him and not tell you and then we'll talk. Until then don't bring that bitch name up to me no more." Dylan spat unfazed by his speech.

"Oh if she fuck Bernard everybody gon' die. But whatever, I tried. If you wanna be mad then that's all on you." Tee-Tee threw up his hand, defeated.

"I'ma let you know now. She will be at my birthday gathering so please be on your best behavior. I don't want no shit on my birthday," Tee-Tee warned.

"If she don't start none it won't be none. I'ma let you know now with all of the stress I've been under as of late that I've been waiting for an excuse to pop a bitch." Dylan put her up dukes and began to fight the air.

"Girl, you ain't Angel. You gon' fuck around and get yo' ass beat. Now c'mon," Tee-Tee linked arms with Dylan. "Lead me back to the kitchen. A bitch is starving."

Time had been going by so fast that almost a month had gone by since Billie last saw Knox's face. He'd call and check up on Kyrese and ask how she was doing but he hadn't stepped foot back into the house since he left. The only reason Billie was able to cope with him being gone was because she gave her full attention and energy to her kids. State being there as a support system was an added bonus.

Since the bath they'd kept it strictly PG. He showed signs of liking her every now and then but Billie didn't concentrate on that. Half the time she didn't know if she was coming or going. Her life was so up in the air. Nothing was set in stone and that scared the holy shit out of her. She was use to having structure in her life. Every since the accident it'd been completely the opposite.

Something had to change so she decided to look up Knox's address and go see him. He hadn't bothered to give her his new address and Billie's pride was too big to ask for it. She thought that gathering up all of his mail would be a good excuse to drop by unannounced. The fact that she was popping up on her husband was utterly ridiculous but this is what her life had become.

Never the one to leave the house without being dressed to the nine's Billie flat ironed her hair bone straight with a part in the middle. She wore a light amount of YSL foundation and powder. A vibrant shade of hot pink lipstick adorned her lips. Covering her eyes were a $500 pair of black Versace shades. Billie was elegant and lady-like in a white Ralph Lauren button up with a light grey crewneck sweater over it. The rest of her outfit consisted of a pair of black cigarette pants, a satin Carolina Herrera floral print baby-doll coat; Alexander McQueen pointed metal-toe pumps and a 3.1 Phillip Lim satchel bag.

Winter was approaching so her outfit was perfect for the chilly mid-western weather. With her bag and mail in hand, Billie rang Knox's doorbell. Apparently he had rented a three story walkup in south St. Louis. From the outside it looked pretty nice. The neighborhood seemed quiet and quaint. Seconds later, Billie heard the sound of someone approaching the door.

"Who is it?" A chipper female's voice asked from the other side of the door.

Caught off guard by the voice, Billie cleared her throat and said, "Mrs. Christianson."

It was mid-day so she wondered why would Knox have a woman over at 12:32 in the afternoon on a Wednesday? Billie got her answer when the door opened and there stood the white girl Knox worked with down at the bar. The same white chick she'd accused him of cheating on her with a year before.

"Hi Billie." Jessica spoke with an uncomfortable expression on her face.

"Is my husband here?" Billie asked, seeing that Jessica wore only a tee shirt.

What made it worse was that the tee shirt belonged to Knox.

"Yes. Come on in." Jessica stepped aside so Billie could enter. "I'll let Knox know you're here." She closed the door and took off running up the steps. "Knox!"

As her heart raced, Billie peeked around the main floor of the house. Knox's home was beautifully decorated. She could tell by how well everything was put together that he hadn't done it by himself. His home had a women's touch to it. The layout was a mixture of Urban Outfitters and Anthropology. Huge pieces of art work covered the walls. The built-in couches were delicately crafted and accented his wooden coffee table well.

A gut full of emotions swarmed through Billie as she waited for Knox to come face her. She was mad. She was livid. She felt betrayed. She felt lied to. She felt like a fool. Here she was holding onto something that was obviously not there anymore. Maybe she deserved to feel the way she felt. She'd done far worse but damn did it hurt. Knox was still her husband.

Had he so easily moved on from her? Now she wondered had she been right all along? Had he and Jessica been having an affair? Billie's temperature rose she was so mad. Knox came down the steps with a v-neck tee shirt in his hand, a pair of jeans on and nothing else. Sex was written all over him. It was apparent to Billie that he and Jessica had just finished doing the do. Once he hit the bottom step, he pulled the shirt on over his head and greeted Billie with a kiss on the cheek.

"How you doing?" He tried to hug her but Billie dodged the hug and stepped away from him.

"What the hell is going on here?" She hissed, pushing him in the center of chest.

"We are not about to do that Billie," Knox replied, calmly.

"Not about to do what?" Billie snapped, rolling her neck.

"I'm not about to argue wit' you. If you wanna talk lets talk but all that extra shit ain't about to go down."

"So let me get this shit straight." Billie stood back on one leg. "You're fuckin' Malibu Barbie, the same Malibu Barbie!" Billie yelled so Jessica could hear her.

"That I accused you of fuckin' a year ago and I don't have the right to be upset? Yo' white ass must be crazy! Are you sleeping with her? You know what?" Billie placed her hand up.

"Don't even answer it 'cause I already know the answer. Of course you're fucking her and you have been for months," she scoffed, throwing his mail at him.

The envelopes hit Knox square in the face then fell to the floor.

"You're right. I am fuckin' her," Knox responded, unapologetically. "You and I both know that our marriage is done. After everything that has happened there ain't no going back. If you could stop being angry for a minute and admit that things would be a lot better."

Deep down Billie knew he was right. Their marriage had been dead for a long time. She didn't love him the way he deserved to be loved. She never had. Billie was incapable of loving any man because her heart belonged to State and State only. She deserved to finally be happy and so did Knox. He'd been a great husband and stepdad to her kids. She couldn't deny him happiness. Yes, it hurt to see him moving on without her but it was for the best.

"How did we get here?" Billie hung her head low. "We were supposed to work but we don't."

"It wasn't meant to be." Knox walked up and hugged her. "I'll always love you and the kids and if you

232

need anything, I'm here. You know that, right?" He squeezed her tight.

"Yeah," Billie sniffled as a single tear slid down her cheek. "I'm sorry for hurting you," she whispered.

"It's all good," Knox released her from his embrace. "No matter what we're still family."

That smile on your face makes it easy for me to trust you.
-Miguel, "The Girl With The Tattoo"

Chapter 17

After having a shitty beginning of the week, Billie counted down the days, hours and minutes until she got to see her girls. Only seeing them every two weeks was killing her softly. Her life hadn't been the same without them. Thank god she had Kyrese and State to occupy her time. Kyrese was fully healed and doing well in school. He was still very recluse and bitter at times towards her. She often wondered how long he'd hate her for the lie she'd told.

It'd been two months since the accident and he still looked at her with disgust in his eyes. Billie prayed it wouldn't last forever. She needed her son back. She needed him to forgive her. She missed how close they once were. Kyrese still hadn't fully warmed up to State either. No matter how hard he tried to build a rapport with him, Kyrese would continuously shut him out.

He was nice and respectful to him but that was about it. It was funny how close she and State had become. The friendship they once shared was in full force again. Whenever he wasn't spending time with Kyrese, State made it his business to see about Billie. They watched movies, ratchet VH1 shows, discussed music and more together. Billie expressed her desire to finally get into the music industry. State agreed that she should follow her dreams.

It was a Friday night. State and Kyrese were in the kitchen taking out ingredients so everyone could make their own personal homemade pizza. Billie thought it would be a fun treat for the kids and State was down. Pandora was on and of course State had it on the hip hop station. Future featuring Pusha T and Pharrell *Move That Dope* was bumping throughout the house, creating a party like atmosphere. The sound of the doorbell ringing caused Billie's heart to skip a beat. Her girls were home! Billie's maid Zoila greeted the girls and Cain at the door.

"Coma esta." Zoila hugged the twins.

"What it do Zoila?" The girls hugged her back.

"My babies!" Billie opened her arms wide for Kaylee and Kenzie to run into.

The girls were elated to see their mother. They missed her tremendously. They loved their father but nothing beat being at home with their mother.

"What in the hell is up wit' ya'll hair?" Billie looked from one daughter to the next.

236

The twins' hair was natural and curly so if you didn't know anything about African American hair the girls could end up looking a hot mess, which they were. Their hair was all over their heads and looked as if it hadn't been combed or moisturized in weeks.

"Chile…" Kaylee slapped her hand against her knee. "It's been a struggle. Them niggas over there can't do nothing right."

"Watch your mouth lil' girl!" Billie pointed her finger in Kaylee's face.

"I'm just saying." Kaylee replied in a ghetto girl tone.

"Yeah, Mama Billie we need you to get our heads together cause I can't continue to walk around like this." Kenzie chimed in. "My lil' boo at school ain't been checking for me all week."

"Girl bye." Billie pushed her to the side. "I'ma deal with you and your sister later." Billie glared towards the door and locked eyes with Cain.

Although she couldn't stand his guts, she couldn't deny that he looked nice. He was casually dressed in an army green Brunello Cucinelli trench coat, white v-neck tee shirt, distressed slim fit Dsquared2 jeans and Lanvin sneakers. The six thousand dollar, Tag Heuer Swiss watch

237

that she'd bought him for their 8th wedding anniversary shown from his wrist. His stylist was styling the hell out of him. Too bad there was no one to rework his piss poor personality.

"Cain." She spoke dryly.

"Cruella." He shot back.

"Grow up." Billie screwed up her face.

"Hey dad!" Kyrese walked up beside his mother and spoke.

Every time Cain dropped the girls off Kyrese was so happy to see him.

"It's Cain now, Kyrese. I've told you that." Cain responded firmly.

"I'm sorry … Cain," Kyrese said, feeling two feet tall. "Can I come over and spend the night next weekend?"

"I don't know if that's a good idea."

"Cain! Are you fucking kidding me?" Billie exploded.

"It's cool, ma." Kyrese shook his head sad and disappointed.

Without uttering another word Kyrese left as quickly as he came. Pissed to the highest level, Billie stormed up into Cain's face.

"What the fuck is wrong wit' you? Why would you do him like that? That boy has gone through hell and back."

"And you're to blame for that," Cain shot.

"Please believe I know that but you mean to tell me he can't come to your house and spend the night with you? Although you're not his biological father, you're still all he knows and Kaylee and Kenzie are his sisters. Separating him from you all is so fuckin' heartless. You really, truly need to check yourself, Cain. Cause if you keep treating him like that God is going to rain down a fireball of hell on you. Now get the fuck off my door step!" Billie slammed the door in his face.

"You tell'em mama!" Kenzie applauded her mother.

"Kenzie Syleena Townsend go sit your ass down somewhere! I am not in the mood!" Billie warned.

"Uh oh time to go!" Kenzie ran back into the kitchen.

Breathing heavily, Billie closed her eyes and willed herself to calm down. She hated that Cain brought out the absolute worst in her but in this case she couldn't contain herself. Nobody fucked with her kids.

"You straight?" State asked, coming into the foyer.

Billie spun around and looked helplessly at him.

"I hate him," she seethed anger.

"No you don't."

"Oh yes the fuck I do." Billie stressed.

"Man fuck that nigga. He don't wanna have nothing to do with Kyrese then fuck him. I'm his father and I'ma make sure he's straight no matter what," State confirmed.

"I hear you but for twelve years all Kyrese has known is Cain. He loves him and he misses him and his sisters. "

"That's understandable but we're gonna make it through this."

"We?" Billie eyed him skeptically.

"Yeah, we nigga. I told you I'm not going no where," State flashed a sexy grin. "Now c'mon these kids are hungry." He pulled her into the kitchen.

Over the next hour Billie, State and the kids created their own personal pizzas. They had an island full of ingredients from spinach, chicken, mushrooms, artichokes, bacon and more. The kids had a ball rolling out their own dough and dancing to the music. All of the kids except Kyrese, he sat off to the side quietly while everyone laughed and danced.

"C'mon Billie show the kids that you know how to Crip walk." State did the infamous west coat dance.

"My mama does not know how to Crip Walk," Kenzie said in disbelief, rolling her neck.

"See ya'll think ya'll know me but you don't!" Billie stood in the center of the floor and twisted her feet in several different directions along to the beat of YG feat Drake *Who Do You Love*. The kids were stunned to see their mother acting so hood. She always was so classy and reserved. She and State Crip Walked with one another and died laughing while doing so.

"They don't know nothing about this!" Billie bust out doing the Kid n Play.

State happily joined in with her.

The kids sat back and looked at them like they were two old dinosaurs.

"C'mon Kenzie, lets show'em how it's done." Kaylee and her sister hopped down from their chairs.

St. Louis own Laudie's *Stripper Bop* was playing. Kaylee and Kenzie bent over and shook their little butts then stood up and bopped like Beyoncé in the Drunk in Love video. Billie couldn't believe her eyes. Her girls were dancing like they were grown ass women on the pole.

"That is enough!" She quickly turned off the stereo. "Where did you all learn that shit from?"

"Mama Boots taught us." Kenzie said out of breath."Ooh I need some water." She fanned herself.

"I'ma kick her ass!" Billie grabbed her car keys.

"You ain't trying to go jail." State took the keys from her hand.

"What kind of woman teaches two eight year olds how to twerk?"

"Mama Boots." Kaylee gave her a mock-glare and grinned.

"You shut up!" Billie advised, pissed.

"Chill out shorty." State wrapped his arm around her waist and pulled her into him. "We not gon' let nothing negative ruin tonight. You only got two days with your girls. Make it count."

Billie massaged her temples with her index fingers. If State wasn't there to calm her down she would've been to Cain's house by now whooping Puss-n-Boots silicone inflated ass. State was the only person to make her think twice before reacting. His strong presence tamed her and she secretly liked it. Besides, he was right. Spending time with her kids was all that mattered.

Billie hadn't felt this much joy in her heart in forever. Whenever her girls were home she felt whole. Her home was meant to be filled with giggles and fun. She wished that everyday could be like that. Life would be so much easier. Once the pizzas were done and out of the wood burning oven, they all sat around the dining table and ate.

"How was school this week?" Billie asked, the girls before taking a bite of her pizza.

"It was a'ight," Kenzie frowned.

"I frankly wasn't there for it." Kaylee smacked her food.

"Why?" Billie questioned, perturbed.

"Cause Mama Boots tried it wit' this hair." Kaylee picked at her hair. "And I got in trouble for talking during class and had to miss recess for two days straight."

"Well, you need to learn how to hush. You can talk during lunch and free time. Not while your teacher is trying to teach class." Billie shot her a death glare.

"Mama you know I'm trying to be the next Wendy Williams or Keisha Ervin. Talking ish is my life!"

"You keep on talking in class and I'ma end yo' life," Billie retorted.

"Mama Billie are you ever gon' stop being a thug?" Kenzie asked, curious.

"Yo' mama been a thug on the low since forever." State laughed at Kenzie's silliness.

243

"Excuse you, there is nothing thuggish about me," Billie sneered.

"Kyrese you like your pizza?" State asked, noticing that he was being very quiet.

"It's cool, I guess." Kyrese shrugged his shoulders.

State looked at his son with sorrow in his eyes. He wanted so badly to make his son happy but nothing that he tried worked. He came by everyday to see him. He helped him every night with his homework, ate dinner with him, tried to spark up conversations with him but Kyrese wasn't willing to open up to him.

"You wanna play NBA 2k13 when we finish eating?" State got his attention.

"I don't care," Kyrese responded, dryly.

Kyrese just wanted to disappear. He didn't want to be there pretending to be one big happy family. All he wanted was to be alone. When he was alone, he had time to day dream about the times when they really were a happy family. When Kyrese was alone in his room he could reminisce on when he and Cain used to play touch football together.

It didn't happen as often as he would've liked but when it did he cherished the moment. Before he learned that Cain wasn't his father he always felt like the odd man out but now it really was his reality. The man he'd known as his father didn't love him. Kyrese had to figure out a way to cope with his new reality but seeing his father with his sisters only magnified his pain.

"Okay girls," Billie wiped her hands on a napkin. "It's bath time."

"Aww man we wanted to kick it wit' Kyrese new daddy some more." Kenzie whined, poking out her bottom lip.

"Maybe if you be a good girl for your mother, she'll let you and sister stay up a little while longer so we all can play Monopoly." State patted Kenzie on the top of her head.

"Okay Kyrese daddy," Kaylee interjected. "We are not five and this ain't the Disney network. Speak hood to us 'cause all that other stuff is killing my vibe."

"Where did these lil' girls come from?" State glanced at Billie shocked.

"I've been asking myself that question since the day they were born." Billie shook her head, slightly embarrassed.

"Mama Billie?" Kaylee tugged on her mother's shirt.

"Yes, Kaylee." Billie prepared herself for some more nonsense.

"Hold onto this one. You got you a winner on your hands. He a cutie." Kaylee winked her eye.

"I have had it!" Billie threw down her napkin. "Get yo' little ass up them damn steps!" Billie pointed towards the staircase.

"Look at what you did." Kenzie pushed her sister. "You always getting us in trouble."

"Shut up lil' ugly girl." Kaylee pushed her back.

"I look just like you!" Kenzie countered.

"Enough!" Billie shrieked. "And no more pushing each other!" She followed them up to their room.

"C'mon Kyrese." State got up from the table. "Let's load the dishwasher."

"Nah, I'm good." Kyrese pushed his plate away from him.

"C'mon man. It'll only take a minute."

"Why?" Kyrese ice grilled him. "Zoila's here. She can do it. It is her job"

"You're right. It is her job but it's nice to help out around the house from time to time."

"Since when you care about helping other people? Your entire career has been built on you being a douche bag." Kyrese stated blunted.

"Ya'll must not get whoopings around here?" State said more as a fact and not a question. "Yo' me and you need to wrap with one another." State sat back down.

"Yeah, I've been known to be a dick. I've made some terrible choices in my life, a lot of which I regret. What you need to know about me is that I don't have a lot of family. The family that I do have, I barely speak to or see. For years all I've had was me and being a loner caused me to think selfishly and behave recklessly. I'm not proud of the things that I have done but now I have you. I want to be a better man for you. I want you to be proud to call me your dad."

"I know you're technically," Kyrese put up air quotes. "suppose to be my father but I don't know you like that nor do I want to."

"Why though?" State died to know.

"Do we have to talk about this? Look, I'll load the damn dishes." Kyrese said becoming upset.

"Yeah 'cause I'm trying to figure out why you won't open to me. I mean, I'm here. I'm trying."

"So! That don't mean nothing!" Kyrese barked. "My daddy … I mean Cain was there for me too and he left so you being here don't mean shit!" Kyrese smacked his plate off the table causing it to break.

Hot tears streamed down his face at lightening speed.

"What was that?" Billie yelled from the top of the steps.

"Nothing!" State shouted back. "I dropped a plate!"

Billie knew when State was lying so instead of heading back to the girls she crept down the steps and listened in on his and Kyrese's conversation.

"Kyrese," State scooted his chair closer to him. "I'm not going nowhere."

"You're lying! You left my mother so what makes you think I don't believe you won't leave me too?" Kyrese's chest heaved up and down.

"I did leave your mom when we were younger and it's a decision that I have regretted every single day of my life. But now I have been given a second chance to make things right with your mother and be a great father to you. We don't know each other like that and I know you may not trust me right now but I swear to you that I'm going to die trying to make you see that I'm here. You're my son

248

and I love you. I'm not Cain. I will never leave you," State said sincerely and truthfully.

"I got you man." State took his son into his arms and hugged him.

In his father's arms Kyrese allowed himself to cry freely. Billie watched from afar and her heart broke and screamed tears of joy for her son. He was finally opening his self up to State and it was good to see them bond on a deeper level.

"I love you, okay?" State kissed Kyrese on the top of his head as he shed a tear.

"Didn't Kaylee tell you this ain't no damn Disney show. You can stop with the dramatics," Kyrese joked, laughing.

"Watch your damn mouth," State said with a laugh.

Darling, you give but can not take love.
-Drake feat Jhene Aiko, "From Time"

Chapter 18

After having a fun filled weekend with all of the kids, the girls returned home to Cain's house. Each time they left it reminded Billie that it would be a full two weeks before she could see them again. The appeal hearing couldn't come soon enough. She had to get her girls back. Until then she would cope with the unfortunate situation the best way she could. On that Monday morning Billie was up and alone with no one to talk to.

Kyrese was at school, Tee-Tee was at work, Zoila was busy cleaning the house and Dylan was still giving her the silent treatment. Billie's entire schedule was clear for the day. She didn't have to be at the art gallery. With nothing to do she decided she'd surprise State with lunch. All weekend he'd been so fantastic with her and the kids. The girls loved him and by the time Sunday rolled around he and Kyrese were buddied up like old friends. He deserved to be treated with a nice meal after all he'd done.

Excited that she had a legit reason to see his face, Billie dialed Wasabi restaurant and placed an order for an array of sushi. The order would be ready in little under an hour so that gave Billie enough time to slip into something fabulous. Billie quickly ransacked her closet and found a sickening outfit. Her hair was up in a bun so she chose an upper eastside of Manhattan inspired ensemble.

Billie wore an orange waist length pea coat, Roland Mouret blue and white striped skater girl dress, Alice + Olivia orange sling back pumps with a single bow off to the side of the back and Proenza Schouler satchel leather bag. Thankfully she had naturally beautiful even skin. All she had to do was throw on a little mascara and some bright red RiRi Woo M.A.C. lipstick and she was ready to go. It took her no time to pick up the food and head over to State's office.

When she reached his floor the receptionist desk was empty so Billie didn't waste anytime bypassing it and walking into State's office unannounced. She had no time to waste. After sitting out for a period of time, sushi would start to fall apart and Billie was too hungry for that to happen. The takeout bag was already too heavy and plus she couldn't wait to see the surprised look on State's face when she entered his office.

Instead of State being surprised, she was the one stunned. As soon as she walked through the threshold of his door she witnessed State standing in the middle of his office hugging a woman. This wasn't any ordinary hug though. It wasn't a cordial, end of a business meeting hug. This was the kind of hug where their bodies were pressed up against one another. His hands were wrapped fully around her waist as they embraced and his eyes were closed like he was savoring the moment.

The chick was bad too. She reminded Billie of the popular makeup artist Amrezy. She was petite with round hips and a fat ass. Billie felt like she had the wind knocked out of her. How could life be repeating itself? No, they weren't an item but he sure had led her to believe that they were building towards something close to it. State opened his eyes and immediately spotted Billie standing there like a deer caught in head lights.

"Billie." He swiftly ended the embrace and stepped away from the woman.

"I'm sorry to have interrupted you." Her face burned from embarrassment. "I was just bringing you some lunch but I guess I caught you at a bad time." Billie placed the food down on the coffee table.

"Nah, you good." State tried to stop her from leaving.

"No," Billie snapped. "I think its best I leave." Her nostrils flared she was so upset.

"Is this *the* Billie?" The woman asked.

"Yes it is," State smiled.

"It's so nice to finally meet you." The woman extended her hand for a shake. "I'm State's receptionist, Essence."

"Nice to meet you." Billie shot her stank look and opted out of her shaking her hand.

"*Okay*," Essence eyes widened. "On that note I'll be heading back to my desk. State call my desk if you need anything." Essence left the room and closed the door behind her.

"What brings you here?" State sat on the edge of his desk.

"I don't have time for this shit," Billie turned to leave with an attitude.

"Where you going? You just got here." State ran behind her and blocked her from leaving.

"I'm so fuckin' stupid," Billie scoffed.

"What are you talking about?"

"Move State," Billie's voice cracked.

"Not until you tell me what your fuckin' problem is."

"I'm not going to ask you again. Move!"

"No," State responded calmly.

"Yo' ass ain't changed," Billie griped. "You're still on the same bullshit you were on in 2002."

"I have no idea what you're talking about." State said thoroughly confused.

"Move! I don't have time for a bunch of back and forth bullshit with you!" Billie tried pushing him out of the way to no avail.

State was ten times bigger and stronger than her. She couldn't move him if she used all of her strength. Instead, State exchanged positions with her and pressed her back up against the door.

"Yo' what the fuck is your problem?" He shot her a look that could kill.

"You! You're my problem! I can't believe that I let you sucker me into believing that we were some type of family!"

"We are."

"You and Kyrese are but me and you—" She pointed back and forth between them. "We ain't shit! I know you fuckin' that bitch! You can't even keep your dick inside your pants for five minutes! Get the fuck out my face!" She tried to open the door but State grabbed the knob before she could.

"Man if you don't stop with that bullshit." He ignored her temper tantrum. "I ain't fuckin' that girl," he laughed.

"And you think the shit is funny?' Billie quipped ready to go off. "If you don't get the fuck off of me you better."

"What you gon' do if I don't?"

Billie ice grilled him.

"Nothing ... exactly," State checked her. "If you would chill the fuck out you would know that I'm not fucking Essence."

"Yeah sure and I'm boo-boo the fool. Tell me anything. State I know you." Billie rolled her eyes.

"You know the old me but obviously not the new me. Essence has been my employee for years and if you paid any attention to her left hand you would've saw that she's married. She and her husband Adam are expecting their first child. She just told me the news. That's why we were hugging."

Billie gazed deep into State's brown eyes. He was telling the truth. Billie felt like a complete and utter fool. Once again she'd led off of anger before receiving all of the facts.

"Now tell me you're sorry," State demanded.

"No," Billie said, stubbornly.

"You always gon' be my little trouble maker," State grinned, sliding his warm hand up Billie's dress.

"What are you doing?" Billie panicked.

"Shhhh." State silenced her with a kiss.

"We are not about to have sex in your office," Billie's heart raced.

"Oh yes the fuck we are." State spun her around and lifted up her skirt.

"State wait," Billie whined.

"Shut up." He ignored her feeble protest.

It' had been twelve years since he had her face down with her ass up in the air. Billie's face was pressed up again the door. State ripped her g string off with one tug. Billie's round ass cheeks jiggled in from of him. State inserted himself deep within her. He still fit perfectly inside her warm slit. State took a deep breath and worked his dick in and out of her pussy.

Each thrust of his dick sent chills up Billie's spine. Never in a million years did she think that she would be here. State still knew all the right spots to hit that would make Billie lose her mind. Only he could take her to the moon and back. There was no more fighting their feelings for one another. They both still cared deeply for another and it was apparent. State was the only man that could take her into orbit. With him she was putty in his hands. State could have her any way he pleased. She was his and he was hers for eternity.

The day was November 17th. Dylan was sound asleep in bed snuggled under her Versace covers when her cell phone rang. Beyonce's *Mine* ringtone let her know that it was Angel calling. Dylan reached for her phone and swiped to the right to answer.

"Morning baby," Angel said in a raspy deep tone.

"Hi baby." Dylan responded groggily. "How was your morning workout?"

"Good. I'm about to go do a sparring session in a minute. I was just trying to call you before you left for the day."

"Thanks baby that was sweet," Dylan smiled, brightly.

"Where my big head boy at?"

"Right here, lying right next to me," Dylan giggled. "I'm surprised I didn't roll over on him." She kissed Mason on the forehead.

"What time is it?"

"Almost eleven," Angel responded.

"Shit! I gotta get up and start getting dressed."

"Aww yeah, today is Tee-Tee birthday, right?"

"Yeah," Dylan massaged the left side of her pelvis.

"Oooh shit," she whimpered. "I'm cramping. Is it time for me to come on my period?"

"I think so," Angel replied, drinking a bottle of water. "How long are you going to be gone?"

"Umm ... I should be back by like seven or eight. The movie starts at 1:30."

"What ya'll going to see?"

"I wanted to go see The Best Man Holiday but you know Tee-Tee ole Chris Hemsworth loving ass wanna see Thor: The Dark World cause he's is in it."

"My god." Angel shook his head.

"Right!"

"Well, it is his birthday."

"Yeah," Dylan held her breath. "I hate I'm cramping though. I hope this shit goes away before I leave."

"You'll be straight but look I gotta go. Kiss my boy for me and I'll see you later."

"Ok, I love you."

"Love you too," Angel ended the call.

By the time Dylan made it to the AMC Dine-In Theater the pain in her pelvis on the left side had gone from a dull pain to a searing sensation. She prayed that by the time the movie was over that the cramping would've stopped. If the cramping hadn't stopped she was going to most definitely stop and pick up some extra strength Midol. She didn't even know how she was able to get dressed let alone drive all the way out to the theater.

Somehow she pulled it together and was able to look camera ready. Dylan had to turn it out for the kids. Tee-Tee's gay friends loved Dylan and her fresh off the runway style. With her short hair freshly died platinum blonde she had to slay the scene in a black Crooks and Castle snapback, diamond stud earrings, gold collar necklace, red Crooks and Castle sweatshirt, Cartier gold men's watch, black leather leggings, Saint Laurent suede peep-toe lace-up booties and a extra sickening red $7750 VBH Brera ostrich satchel bag.

Dylan had her makeup artist Keisha give her an ultra sexy but simple beat. She had a black cat-eye with a set of mink lashes and a ruby red lip. Dylan was serving up designer b-girl glamour and loving it. Due to her not feeling well she was the last one to arrive to the movie theater. Tee-Tee, Bernard and Billie were there as well as Tee-Tee's friends, I Woke Up Like Dis, Delicious, Shiver-Me-Tender, Cheri Bomb, Rhea Listic and Clara Tin.

The girls were all in full drag and serving up a heavy dose of video vixen realness. However none of the queens outshined Tee-Tee. He'd gone all out for his birthday. He wore the hell out of a full length crème colored fox fur, white mini freak'um dress and Christian Louboutin multi-colored Pigalle spiked pumps. To set the entire look off a pair of Balenciaga transparent aviator shades covered his.

"Bitch!" Tee-Tee snapped his finger. "If you make me miss one second of Chris Hemsworth without his shirt on its gon' be me and you!"

"You better be glad I don't feel good and that it's your birthday 'cause I am not in the mood for your shenanigans today." Dylan gave him a warm hug. "Happy birthday, baby."

"Thank you, suga." Tee-Tee beamed, smiling from ear to ear.

"Hey everybody." Dylan waved to the group then threw up the middle finger to Billie.

Everyone spoke back not aware that Dylan wasn't joking with Billie.

"Hi to you too Dylan." Billie said taken aback by her behavior.

Dylan could tell that Billie was uncomfortable and nervous to be around her. Dylan being Dylan wasn't in the mood to play nice. She hadn't seen Billie in months and actually preferred it that way. Being in her presence only reminded her of all of the lies and deceit. She didn't care if she'd hurt Billie's feeling. She wanted her to feel like crap.

"You okay?" Delicious their hairstylist asked Billie.

He knew the inside tea on the entire demise of Billie and Dylan's friendship.

"Yeah," Billie lied swallowing the huge lump in her throat.

"Okay 'cause we can jump her," Delicious joked, wrapping his arm around her shoulder.

Together they walked in. While watching the movie all Dylan could concentrate on was the pain in her pelvis. She couldn't wait for the movie to be over so she could get some medication to sooth the pain. After almost two hours of super powers, sword fighting and muscle bound bodies the movie was over and the entire group piled out of the theater. Dylan was in so much pain that she couldn't even stand up straight.

She'd never cramped like this before. She had to stop on the way to the bowling alley to get some Midol. Once she got it she took two pills with a bottle of water, praying that the retched pain would disappear. Unfortunately for Dylan, by the time she made it into the city the pain had magnified. The pain she was feeling was the equivalent of child birth.

She knew she should call it a day and head home but it was Tee-Tee's birthday and she had to be there with him to celebrate. He'd been there for her during every milestone of her life. It was only fair that she be there for him during his. As Dylan parked her 2014 Mercedes Benz SLS-Coupe in the parking lot of the Flamingo Bowl she felt something pop on her lower left side. The sudden sensation caused her to press her foot on the brake and grab her stomach. She didn't know what was happening. The Midol wasn't working and all she wanted was to lie down but the gang was waiting on her once again. Dylan sucked up the pain, grabbed her purse and got out of the car.

"You look like shit." Tee-Tee screwed up his face. "Are you alright?"

"Does it look like I'm okay? I'm cramping like a muthafucka and I just felt something pop in my stomach." Dylan replied hunched over.

"Girl, you need to go home."

"No," Dylan waved him off. "I'm alright. C'mon lets go inside. I'm dying for a slice of pizza."

"Okay," Tee-Tee eyed her skeptically.

Forty-five minutes into bowling the pizza had come and Dylan was in even worse shape. It took the will of God and Blue Ivy for her to stand up to bowl each time it was her turn. Somehow she was able to manage but after a while she couldn't pretend like everything was okay anymore. Sweat poured from her forehead and she'd begun to feel dizzy. It was time for her to go home and rest.

"Tee-Tee I'm sorry but I gotta go," she winced.

"You need me to drive you home?" He asked, truly concerned.

"No, I'll make it." Dylan tried to convince herself.

"Are you sure? 'Cause I will drive you." Billie chimed in.

She didn't care about Dylan's beef with her. Dylan looked like she'd been through a battle and lost all while wearing designer duds. She was obviously sick and needed

264

help. Despite Dylan's feelings towards her, Billie was going to offer her assistance.

"I'm fine," Dylan groaned, annoyed by the sound of Billie's voice. "Tee-Tee, I'll call you later. Ya'll have a good time." Dylan eased herself out of the bowling alley and back to her car.

It was purely by the grace of God that she got home safely. Dylan never despised the long staircase in her home more. She stood exasperated at the bottom of the stairwell wondering how she was going to make it up. The entire room was spinning and sweat poured from every crevice her body.

It seemed like it took her a century to get from the bottom of the staircase and up to her room. By the time she reached her bed, Dylan was covered in sweat. She was extremely dizzy and in desperate need of lying down. Quickly she stripped down to nothing but her panties and got underneath the covers.

"Jaime!" Dylan pressed the intercom next to her bed. "Can you please make me a rice sock," Dylan said wearily.

"Yes ma'am," Jaime responded back.

A few minutes later Jaime entered Dylan's master bedroom with a hot rice sock in her hand.

"Is everything okay Mrs. Carter?" Jaime handed her the rice sock.

"I'm having really bad menstrual cramps. I hope this rice sock helps." Dylan took it from her and placed it under her stomach.

"It's time for me to go home now. Do you need me to stay?"

"I hate to ask but can you please stay at least until Mr. Carter gets home," Dylan pleaded, barely able to speak.

"Yes of course," Jaime agreed. "I'll give Mason his bath and put him to bed. I hope you feel better and let me know if you need anything else."

"Thank you Jaime. Can you please close the door behind you?"

In extreme agony, Dylan placed the rice stomach on the left side of her pelvis. The warm sensation helped soothe the ache somewhat but not enough to stop Dylan from crying out to God for help.

I don't wanna lose you now I'm lookin' right at the other half of me.
-Justin Timeberlake, "Mirror"

Chapter 19

By ten o'clock that night Angel came home to find his wife lying on her stomach. Her pillow was soaked with tears.

"Baby, I got here as quick as I could. What's wrong?" He sat next to her on the bed.

"I don't know if I'm cramping or what but I've been hurting since I woke up this morning. I took some Midol but that didn't work at all. I don't know what's wrong with me," Dylan sobbed.

"You wanna go to the emergency room?" Angel ran his fingers through her hair.

"I don't wanna go sit in a waiting room for hours if it's only menstrual cramps."

"But you don't know if that's all it is," Angel said, concerned.

"I did feel something pop earlier on my left side," Dylan confessed.

"That don't sound right, babe." Angel lie next to his wife and held her close. "You sure you don't want to go to the emergency room?"

"I'ma wait. If I'm still hurting in the next few hours, I'll go."

"Okay well let's go to sleep for a while." Angel closed his eyes and prayed to god that his wife would feel better.

By 2:00a.m the torture Dylan was in still remained. The pain hadn't gotten any better or any worse. Needing to pee, she eased her way out of the bed. Angel was in a deep sleep so she tried her best not to wake him. Dylan held her side and made her way to the bathroom. She still couldn't even stand up straight. At that point she'd had enough.

After she used the bathroom it was time to go to the hospital. Dylan and Angel sat in the waiting room at Saint Mary's hospital for well over two hours before she was seen. When she finally was seen the nurse asked her to take a urine test. As soon as they asked her to take the test thought that she might be pregnant entered Dylan's mind. The last time she'd felt this kind of pain was when she was pregnant with Mason.

Oh my god, that's it. I'm pregnant, Dylan thought to herself as she pee'd into the cup. If she was pregnant she'd gladly accept the pain she was in any day. When she returned to the waiting room Angel noticed the huge smile spread across her face.

"Baby," she smiled, brightly through the pain.

"What?" He eyed her raising one eyebrow.

"I think I may be pregnant."

"What would make you think that?"

"Cause the last time I was in this kind of pain was when I was pregnant with Mason and I fainted." Dylan made him remember.

"You really think that's what it is?"

"I mean it might be. That's the only thing I can think of." She massaged her left side. "Lord please let me pregnant," Dylan said a prayer to god.

Thirty minutes passed by before the nurse called Dylan to the back to give her lab results. Dylan sat anxiously awaiting the results. She was the edge of her seat. Visions of being a mommy again made all the pain she'd endured worth while.

"Okay Mrs. Carter." The nurse sat opposite of Dylan with the results in her hand. "We have your lab results and you're not pregnant nor do you have a urine infection."

Dylan sat quietly and collected herself before speaking. All of her hopes and dreams had been shattered within a matter of seconds. For months she and Angel had been trying to get pregnant. She'd thought they'd finally reached their goal. She just knew that she was pregnant. She would've even betted money on it. For a second she'd begun to envision her next beautiful caramel baby that would look like either her or Angel. Now she had to put those dreams on hold and figure out what the hell was wrong with her.

"What we want to do now is an X-Ray to see exactly where this pain is coming from. We had to make sure you weren't pregnant first before we performed this procedure." The nurse clarified.

Dylan was in so much distress that she had to be wheeled to the X-Ray room. She prayed to god that the pain would miraculously go away so she could return home to her baby. She hadn't seen him in almost twenty-four hours. Inside the X-Ray room the nurse helped Dylan remove her top and bra. With the assistance of the nurse, Dylan stood up so they could get a clear X-Ray of her stomach and pelvis.

Standing up for Dylan felt like she was being repeatedly kicked in the pit of her stomach with a steel toe boot. She couldn't wait to sit back down. When she sat the pain lessoned. Once the X-Ray was over, Dylan was wheeled back to the triage area, where she was given a robe to put on. Angel was there nervously awaiting her return.

"You okay?" He asked her helping her out of her clothes.

"No," Dylan replied slipping her arms inside the ugly hospital gown. "Green is not my color." She rolled her eyes at the raggedy gown.

"How this gown looks is the least of your worries, pretty girl." Angel helped her up into the hospital bed.

Dylan lie in agony awaiting the X-Ray results when a doctor came in and said they now wanted to do a CT scan on her. Angel and Dylan locked eyes. It was apparent that something serious was wrong with her. The question still remained what was the problem? Dylan was now drowning in fear. She'd never had a CT scan done before so she didn't know what to expect. Moments later she was lying on her back on a narrow bed with a needle being stuck into her vein.

She was warned that the iodine being placed into her system would make her entire body feel hot and could cause shortness of breath. Dylan swallowed hard and prepared herself for the worst. The nurse pressed a button and the doughnut shaped machine she lay before came on. Dylan was told to inhale and hold her breath when the red light above her head came on. As she held her breath, a warm sensation ran through her body. At first it was warm like a sip of hot cocoa on a cold winter's day but then the feeling went from warm to scorching hot.

Dylan had never experienced anything like it before. She kind of liked how the iodine made her feel but still wanted the process to be over soon. *Lord, please don't let anything bad be wrong with me,* she prayed. Once the CT scan was complete, Dylan was back with Angel inside her triage room. Angel being the loving husband he was held her hand. Angel was worried sick out of his mind.

He'd never seen Dylan so sickly. He'd given the world to make her feel better. They'd been in the emergency room for almost six hours. It was going on 8:00a.m and no answer had been given as to what was wrong with her. All of the nonstop drama in his family was driving Angel nuts. They needed peace and fast.

"Mrs. Carter." The doctor entered her room.

"Yes," Dylan answered, eagerly.

"We have all your test results back and it looks like you have perforated your colon."

"What does that mean?" Dylan asked confused.

"It means you have a small hole in your colon." The doctor explained.

"What?!" Dylan and Angel both said at the same time.

"How do I have a hole in my colon?" Dylan's heart rate increased.

"You have diverticulitis. Diverticulitis is a condition that happens when pouches form in the wall of your colon. If the pouches get inflamed or infected, they will burst, in which one of yours did."

"So why do I feel the pain in my pelvis? Why does it feel like cramps?"

"The pain is actually coming from the left lower quadrant of your stomach. You feel most of the pain from there, don't you?" The doctor touched her stomach.

"Yes," Dylan nodded.

"Explain to me doc." Angel jumped in. "How do you get diverticulitis?"

"The cause is actually unknown. Some studies show that a lack of dietary fiber is the cause but there are other studies that disagree with this theory." The doctor clarified.

"So Dylan since you perforated your colon we're going to have to perform emergency surgery on you to prevent the waste in your intestines from spilling into your stomach. You better thank god that you came in when you did. You could've died if you didn't."

Dylan looked at her husband and immediately started to cry. The mere thought of her possibly dying scared her to death.

"We're going to have our resident physician, Dr. Eagan perform the surgery on you to repair the damage to your colon. You'll be going in for surgery within the next hour." The doctor said before leaving the room.

"I'm scared." Dylan sobbed into her hands.

"I know you are baby." Angel shed a single tear too.

Dylan was a natural born fighter. She was strong, yet fragile though. She was the type of woman that could only handle but so much. Angel couldn't handle seeing his wife in such a vulnerable state. The sight shook him to the core.

"It's gonna be okay, pretty girl." He wrapped her up into his arms.

"What if something goes wrong?"

"Don't even speak that shit into existence. You're going to be fine. A week from now we're going to be sitting back laughing at this shit."

"I hope so," Dylan whimpered.

"You gon' be straight. I'm going to be right here with you, okay? I'll be the first person you see when you wake up," Angel promised.

Dylan was in and out of consciousness for a day before she was finally fully awake. Her surgery was a success and without any complications. Throughout the entire five and a half hour surgery Angel was on pins and needles. Outside of his nephew, he never had a loved one in the hospital under severe conditions. The whole time he did nothing but pace back and forth and pray. The reality that he could possibly lose his best friend, partner, lover, confidant and wife was simply unbearable.

Dylan was his world. Without her life wasn't worth living. Without her, he was nothing. He hadn't and would never love another woman the way he loved her. Despite her sometimes ditzy behavior she was the best decision he'd ever made. When they exchanged vows he'd promised to protect her from all harm but Angel couldn't protect her from this.

He couldn't buy his way out of this either. Only God could heal this situation and thankfully he had. It freaked Angel out to see Dylan lying in the hospital bed with her hair all over her head. There was an oxygen mask on her face, heart monitor patches on her chest and an IV needle in her arm. There were so many machines hooked up to Dylan that it frightened him. It was bad enough that after surgery she was placed in ICU. Angel thanked his lucky stars that Billie, Tee-Tee and Candy were there to help comfort and keep him sane. He'd broken down twice after witnessing Dylan in such a helpless state.

Dylan squirmed in her sleep and allowed her eyes to flutter open. Opening her eyes she swallowed the saliva in her throat and felt a tube hit her esophagus. The feeling and the sight of seeing Billie's big face irritated the hell out of her. Dylan had bigger fish to fry though. She could feel that her stomach was bandaged up. The worst part was over. She'd survived surgery. *Thank you lord, I'm alive,* she thought.

"Angel, where is my baby?" She reached out her hand for him.

"The nanny has him. He's okay. You have nothing to worry about, pretty girl." Angel assured, placing a small kiss on the outside of her hand.

"Did the doctor fix my stomach?"

Angel glanced over his shoulder at Candy. Candy willed herself not to cry and placed her head down. Dylan caught the exchange and noticed the worried look on her mother's face.

"Yeah, they fixed it," Angel replied, cautiously.

"Mrs. Carter?" Dr. Eagan walked inside her room.

Dr. Eagan was a short, stout, old, white man with gray hair in the form of a comb-over and wore glasses.

"Yes," Dylan coughed.

"Your surgery went well. As you know we placed you under general anesthesia. I made an incision in your abdomen, removed the diseased section of your large intestine and then I took the two healthy ends and sewed them together."

"Okay."

"Can everyone expect for Mr. Carter step out of the room? I want to take a look at Mrs. Carter's stomach."

"Sure." Everyone nodded and left out.

"Let's see here," Dr. Eagan pulled up the right side of Dylan's gown. "Good, you're not bleeding out." He checked the bandage going down the center of her stomach.

Dylan immediately realized that she would have a huge scar going down the center of her stomach for the rest of her life. There would be no more bikini's or crop tops for her.

"What is this hanging from the right side of my stomach?" She asked alarmed.

There was a medium size clear ball attached to a tube hanging from an opening in her stomach.

278

"That is a drain. We have that there to drain any excess fluids from out of your abdominal cavity. In order to close your incision we stitched your stomach closed from the inside and placed staples and sutures on the outside. Now let's take a look over here." Dr. Eagan pulled up the left side of her gown.

Dylan instantly spotted a clear bag with what looked like a chunk of chicken fat hanging out of her stomach inside of it.

"What the hell is that?" She asked, about to pass out.

"Baby, calm down." Angel tried to soothe her.

"No! What the fuck is this hanging out of my stomach?" Dylan shrieked.

"You all haven't told her?" Dr. Eagan questioned Angel.

"No. We didn't know how to."

"Didn't know how to tell me what?" Dylan quipped, panicking.

"Well Dylan, we had to also perform a colostomy on you," Dr. Eagan, explained.

"What is that?" Dylan furrowed her brows.

"A colostomy is performed when the bowel has to be relieved of its normal digestive work as it heals. A colostomy implies creating a temporary opening of the colon on the skin surface and the end of the colon is passed through the abdominal wall and a removable bag is attached to it. The waste is collected in the bag. That is what you have. What you're looking at is called a colostomy bag which you'll have to have for the next three to six months."

Should we just pretend that love ain't closing in?
-Raheem Devaughn, "Where I Stand"

Chapter 20

Never in Dylan's life did she envision her first Thanksgiving as a newly married woman in the hospital. She'd been at Saint Mary's in the ICU for five days. She hadn't eaten a thing yet. To make matters worse she'd gotten her period and was dealt another shocking blow. Not only would she have to have a colostomy bag for probably six months but while performing her surgery Dr. Eagan noticed that her ovaries were enlarged.

He'd shown Dylan and Angel pictures of her ovaries and they were the size of tennis balls. Dylan was mortified. Once she was well enough she was told that she must see her OB/GYN to find out why her ovaries were that size. After learning the horrific news, Dylan was emotionally done. She couldn't handle anything else negative. In her eyes her life was over.

There was no way she could have a colostomy bag for six days let alone almost six months. How was she going to function with having to shit through her stomach? It was gross. She didn't know how to apply a unit to her stomach and didn't want to take the time to learn how to either. All Dylan could do was cry. None of Angel's inspirational speeches or prayers made her feel any better. She was sick of being confined to the twin sized bed.

She was sick of having a million tubes stuck to her body. The electronic compression stockings strapped to her legs that helped prevent blood clots was working her nerves. She was over peeing through a catheter. She'd only seen her baby once since being in the hospital and was having major motherly withdrawal symptoms. Dylan had never been away from her son so long but it was for the best. She didn't want to risk him getting sick coming to the hospital.

On top of missing her son her career hung in the balance. She had a show to film and by the looks of the things Dylan wasn't heading home anytime soon. *Lord, how did I go from thinking I was having menstrual cramps to thinking I was pregnant, to this?* For that brief moment when she thought she was pregnant Dylan was the happiest she'd been in a long while. All of her hopes and dreams seemed to be aligning. But she wasn't pregnant and it would be a lifetime before she could even think about trying to conceive another child.

Dylan looked over at her husband. Angel hadn't left her side for one second just like he'd promised. Each and every day he sat along side her bed making sure she was okay. He looked so peaceful as he slept on a cot. Dylan told him that he could go home and rest but Angel refused. There was no way he was leaving his girl. His dedication to her made her love him all the more.

She just prayed that they'd be able to survive as she recovered from this unfortunate illness. Dylan grabbed the remote attached to her bed that controlled her bed and television so she could turn the channel when Billie walked in. She hadn't seen her since she'd woke from her surgery. Dylan was too high off pain meds and the shocking news of all her ailments to really trip off Billie being there that day.

She didn't have the time nor the energy for Billie and her drama. But after everything Dylan had gone through she was over being mad. She'd almost died. She didn't have the energy to be upset with Billie anymore.

As a matter of fact as soon as Dylan saw Billie's face her eyes began to well up. No matter how much she denied it over the last few months she missed the hell out of her friend. Sure, she'd betrayed her trust in the worst possible way but now none of that mattered. She could've died and now that she saw how precious life was Dylan didn't want to waste anymore time holding onto silly grudges.

"Billie." Dylan's chest heaved up and down.

"Aww please don't cry." Billie chocked up, rushing over to her friends side.

She'd been dreaming of this moment for months. For a minute there she thought she'd never get her friend back. Dylan had made it crystal clear that she hated her. Billie thought their friendship was over. It crushed her entire heart to see her friend, her sister-in-law so broken and helpless. Dylan didn't deserve this kind of torture.

"I was so scared to come see you again. I didn't think you would want to see me." She held Dylan close.

"I didn't but when have you ever did anything I've told you to do," Dylan joked, still crying.

"I'm so sorry, Dylan, for everything. I never meant to hurt you." Billie held her friend tight.

"I know."

The two friends held each other in silence and let their hearts do all of the talking. Nothing would break them apart. They were friends for life.

"Billie, I'm so scared," Dylan confessed. "Why is this happening to me? I can't deal with all of this."

"Yes, you can. You're strong Dylan. You're stronger than you think."

"No, I'm not," Dylan cried.

Her tears melted into Billie's coat.

"I can't do this. I can not have a freakin' colostomy bag. So what now, I'm supposed to replace my Chanel bag for a colostomy bag," Dylan joked.

"Yes, god is trying to teach you something and in due time you will figure it out."

"I don't want to figure it out though," Dylan pouted. "I want my life back."

That Thanksgiving for Billie had been the best and the worst Thanksgiving she'd ever had. It was the best because she had her friend back. She and Dylan talked for hours while Angel got his much needed rest. Billie caught her up on her custody battle with Cain and Kyrese warming up to State. She conveniently left out the part about her and State rekindling their romance. With all that Dylan had going on she didn't want to drop that bombshell on her and risk them being on bad terms again.

She was so thrilled to have Dylan back that she wasn't going to rock the boat. The most important thing to Billie was being there for Dylan and helping her through this rough time. The downside to Thanksgiving was not having her entire family all together for the holiday. Dylan was in the hospital. Angel was there with her and the twins were with Cain.

After being with Dylan all afternoon she made it over to State's penthouse apartment. Billie loved going over to State's house. He had a 24 hour doorman, indoor and outdoor basketball court, bowling alley, squash court and more. They spent the most of their time between his place and hers.

"Hey there little troublemaker," he said, opening the door.

"Hi," Billie placed a soft kiss on his cheek.

"You got here just in time for Thanksgiving dinner." State took her coat as she walked in.

"It smells delicious in here. Who cooked 'cause I know you didn't?" Billie teased.

"Actually me and the boy did."

"Yeah mom, while you hating. We spent all day in the kitchen cooking this meal," Kyrese teased, taking off his apron.

"Uh oh let me find out I got a mini Bobby Flay on my hands." Billie kissed her son on the cheek.

"You ready to eat?" State asked, setting the table.

"Yes, I am starving. Today has been a long day."

"How is Dylan doing?"

"She's not handling this well at all. You know Dylan is all about her looks and her appearance so this happening to her has traumatized her. She is freaking out."

"Can I go see Auntie Dylan?" Kyrese asked.

"I don't think she wants you to see her yet." Billie replied, somberly.

"Aye man," State tugged on the back of Kyrese's neck playfully. "Let me holla at your mom real quick."

"Okay but no kissing. That mess is gross."

"If you don't get yo' butt out of here." Billie jokingly kicked him in the behind on his way out of the kitchen.

"So Dylan didn't cuss you out?" State quizzed placing the food onto the table.

"Surprisingly no. As soon as she saw me she just broke down and cried." Billie took a seat at the table.

"I feel so bad for Dylan. That's my homegirl. Man I wish there was something I could do to help."

"Wow."

"We ended up talking for hours."

"Did you tell her about us?' State asked.

"No. It wasn't the right time and anyway I didn't know there was an us," Billie quipped, pursing her lips together.

"What you call it? We spend almost everyday with each other. I stay fucking the shit outta you. We're raising our son together so I would think we're an us," State checked her.

"That's what your mouth say but let's not forget that we've been here before. I'm not about to fully invest myself in you only for you to break my heart again, no sir." Billie shook her head.

State came over and stood before her.

"Look at me," he demanded.

Billie did as she was told and looked up at State.

"How many times do I have to tell you that shit is in the past? I'm not a kid anymore. I'm a grown ass muthafuckin' man. I lost you once and I'm not trying to lose you again. You're the one for me. It's always been you. The reason it didn't work out for me and Dylan or me and Ashton is because neither of them were you."

Billie's heart fluttered like a butterflies wings. For years she and State had been fighting their feelings for one another. Now here he was placing his entire soul in the palm of her hand. As she stared into her eyes she knew his

289

words were true. He wanted her like she wanted him. Only he could send her to the moon. With him she kissed the stars. Like him there was no other for her. He was her one.

"What do I have to do to make you see that, I'm not going no where?" State took her by the hand and pulled her into him.

"Do I have to place my lips upon yo' thick thigh? I mean, say baby. Can I be yo' slave? I've got to admit, girl. You're the shit girl and I'm diggin' you like a grave." State quoted A Blue's For Nina (Brotha To The Night) poem from the movie Love Jones.

"You have officially lost your damn mind," Billie laughed uncontrollably.

"Is that a smile me put on your face chile?" State grinned, wickedly.

Billie looked at him and shook her head.

"Okay that didn't work so do I have to put a ring on it?"

"No," Billie continued to laugh. "We are no where close to marriage and besides that I'm still married."

"Fuck yo' husband. I ain't worried about him. I'm the blues in yo' left thigh, tryin' to become the funk in yo' right." State placed a trail of sensual kisses along the nape of her neck.

State's lips reminded her of the richest velvet. Everything about him was hypnotizing. He was fine as fuck. His body was ridiculous and he always knew the right words to say at the right moment. The fact still remained that once upon a time she and State had it all. Maybe they could have it all again. Billie just couldn't risk being toyed with. Many times before he'd claim love to only leave a trail of broken hearts behind him. Billie was too old to be added to that list yet again.

She didn't have time for an emotional rollercoaster. The memory of him leaving her and treating her like he'd never felt her affection still haunted her each time they embraced. How could she so easily trust that he'd never leave her for dead again?

But then State caressed her cheek with the back of his hand. Together they slow danced to a melody that only existed between the two of them. Billie laid her head on his chest. To be with him was like being kissed by god. She wouldn't trade the memory they were creating for all of the gold in the world. Then out of nowhere State began to sing.

"They say all good things fade, looking at my past ain't right,

But I swear you came way, like an angel fell from
the sky, no lie,
Loving you the way you are, made a place in my
heart for love,
And I could never see us falling apart,
We got that kind of fix it up kind of love,
And girl, I don't mind giving you nothing,
Cause in the lowest point of my life,
You made a nigga feel like he's something."

Only a few people knew that State could sing. It was a part of him that he shared with very few. Dylan didn't even know he could sing. His voice was like a jazz horn easy and sweet.

"That was beautiful." Billie caressed the back of his head and gazed lovingly into his eyes.

"I meant every word. I love you Billie. We are a family. I got you. You my baby. I'm here to stay." He swore.

"Fuck it," she replied, tired of running.

"I love you too." She parted her lips and kissed him deeply and passionately.

"Uh hmm," Kyrese cleared his throat. "Are you two done cup-cakin'? The food is getting cold."

You're my end and my beginning.
-John Legend, "All Of Me"

Chapter 21

Christmas and New Years had passed. It'd been a month and half since Dylan's surgery. Since she'd been home she'd been on constant bed rest. The only time she left her bed was to brush her teeth, bathe, empty her bag and go to the doctor. Dylan had never seen more doctors in her life. Every other week she was back and forth to a different physician. Before she left the hospital she had to get the drain from her stomach removed.

The experience was painful and had scared Dylan for life. Having a tube pulled from her stomach was some Sci-Fi movie type bullshit. A week later, half of her staples were removed along with all of the sutures. A week after that the rest of the staples were pulled out. Going to the doctor was a task all in itself. Dylan never knew how much she needed her core until she couldn't use it anymore.

Her stomach was so weak and she was so drained from the surgery that it took her five minutes to get up a flight of stairs and another five minutes to get back down. Dylan hated being so helpless. She could barely walk. She couldn't bathe herself or fix herself a meal. She had to change her entire eating habits. She couldn't drink soda as much; eat chocolate, certain shell fish or red meats. Learning how to change her unit was another hard task for her.

The sight of the portion of her intestine that stuck out of her stomach made her sick. To actually see her go number 2 through her stomach into a plastic bag constantly made her want to throw up. Lord, help her if she developed diarrhea. Diarrhea was a demon within itself. On one occasion while cleaning out her bag Dylan didn't move fast enough and ended up shitting on her big toe. She screamed and cried for nearly an hour afterwards.

It sucked that she had to sleep on her back. Everyday she was in constant back pain. It broke her heart even more that she couldn't hold her baby. Dylan was too afraid that he'd kick her in the stomach on accident. She could only spend time with him from afar. It truly killed her not to be able to hold her son. He was her world.

Since her surgery it was like he was being raised by Jamie and Angel. Dylan didn't want another woman playing mommy to her son on a full-time basis. She normally had her son with her at all times. Now everything was different. Dylan was confined to her bed twenty-four hours of the day. She wasn't able to work. She and Angel weren't intimate on any level.

He slept on one side of the bed and she the other. Everyday he had to bathe her and clothe her. He helped Dylan change her units. Outside of playing her home health care provider all they did was talk. When he was off working, Dylan was left alone with only her thoughts. She was worried sick that her marriage was heading towards splitsville. What kind of wife was she when she couldn't even take care of her household, her baby or other wifely duties?

It was as if she and Angel were slowly becoming roommates. There was no way he could possible find her attractive. All she wore were pajamas and a scarf on her head. She wasn't able to please him sexually. They couldn't go anywhere. Dylan knew that Angel loved her but not enough to put up with all of this crap. In her mind she'd become a charity case. They were only a month and a half into her recovery from the first surgery and still had another one to go. According to the doctors Dylan's reversal surgery wouldn't be until that May.

Dylan didn't know how they would survive another four and a half months of her being an incompetent wife and mother. Angel was sure to get bored and start to look at her like the pathetic woman she'd become. Dylan hated looking at herself in the mirror. To her she'd become ugly. Her reflection in the mirror was unbearable. The old, beautiful, confident, fly Dylan was dead and gone. The scar that was etched into her stomach reminded her that she was sickly.

At one time she could compare her body to any super model on the runway. Now Dylan's body was scarred and marked for life. There was nothing sexy or appealing to her now. Angel could have any woman on the planet there was no way he was going to stay with her. That night they lie in bed. Saturday Night Live was on. Drake was the host. Dylan laid in her usual spot in her and Angel's king size bed.

He lay across the foot of the bed on his iPad. This was how they spent their Saturday nights now. There was no more turn up. Usually they'd be in the club poppin' bottles and vibing out to the music. Dylan could almost bet Angel didn't want to be stuck at home with her. He wasn't the one sick. She was. He didn't have to suffer because of her.

"Babe if you wanna go out wit' your homeboys tonight you can. I won't be mad," Dylan reasoned.

"I told you, I'm good." Angel responded, never once taking his eyes off his iPad.

Dylan picked up on the fact that Angel never looked her directly in the eye anymore. She couldn't really blame him. She barely wanted to look at herself.

"Angel, I know you. You don't want to be here. It's Saturday, go kick it." She pleaded, feeling horrible that he felt obligated to stay at home with her.

"Babe, I'm fine. I'm kicking it wit' you. The club gon' be there."

"Are you sure?"

"Yes," Angel chuckled. "What's the deal? I feel like you got something on your mind, pretty girl." He placed his iPad down and gave her his full attention.

"Nothing about me right now is pretty so you can stop calling me that," Dylan declared.

"What are you talking about?" Angel asked, stunned by her comment.

"Angel," Dylan glared at him. "Let's not fake and front. I'm ugly. I know it and you know it. There is no need to sugarcoat the shit. I mean look at me." Dylan spread out her arms.

"For over a month I've been in nothing but sweats. My hair hasn't been done since god knows when. I need a perm like Ciara need a hit record. Nothing about me screams pretty. More like homeless."

"You tripping."

"Noooo I'm not. I see things quite clearly. I get that you tell me that I'm pretty to make me feel good about myself but it actually makes me feel worse 'cause I know it's not true. You're just saying it because that's the polite thing to do."

"I tell you you're pretty 'cause that's how I honestly feel," Angel said, truthfully. "I don't know what you're looking at but from where I'm sitting I see a woman that despite her circumstances is still fine as fuck. You don't need on a Chanel fit, your hair down or a ton of makeup on for me to find you beautiful. You're beautiful to me with or without those things."

"Look at us though," Dylan's eyes welled up with tears. "It's like we're buddies now. We don't kiss. We barely hug. We don't fuck. We don't make love. I'm no good to you. We haven't even discussed the fact that I just had a test ran to see if I have colon cancer or that my OB/GYN found Dermoid cysts in each of my ovaries and that I might have to have my ovaries removed. Dr. Baum said she won't be able to know if she'll be able to salvage any part of my ovaries until they perform surgery. What if

299

they can't salvage them? What if I can't have anymore kids?" Dylan's bottom lip trembled.

"Stop that," Angel demanded. "We have Mason. It's not like we don't have any kids at all."

"But you know how much I wanted to have another child. Hell, I know how much you wanted another baby."

"I do but your health comes first. Us having another baby doesn't mean shit if you're not here with me to help raise it."

"I just don't want you to leave me," Dylan finally admitted.

"Man shut up," Angel laughed. "We're in this for life. This right here ain't nothing but a test and on everything that I love we gon' pass it with flying colors. Me and you not being able to have sex for a few months is minor. That doesn't lessen my love for you. I've actually grown to love you even more now than I thought I physically could. The conversations we've been having lately has brought me closer to you, Dylan," he assured.

"I need for you to see that you have more to offer than just your outer appearance. You're beautiful inside and out. You have a beautiful mind, a beautiful heart and a beautiful spirit. You're my baby and you always will be. We gon' ride this shit out together, ya' feel me?"

"Okay," Dylan nodded like a little girl.

"And don't ever doubt my love for you again," Angel warned. "If you do I'ma kick yo' pretty ass all over St. Louis."

By March, Dylan was up and running. She'd gotten her strength back and was able to feed and bathe herself again. The test results to determine whether she had colon cancer came back negative. Dylan thanked god, Blue Ivy, Tupac, Biggie, Left Eye and Aaliyah for the blessing. She was also thankful that she was 100% back into mommy mode. Being at home with her son on a daily basis was the greatest gift she'd received from god. She'd forgotten how being a working mom took up so much of her time.

Although Mason was there with her everyday on set, Dylan wasn't mentally and emotionally as in check with him as she should've been. Having the opportunity of being home with him changed all of that. She enjoyed every minute of quality time that she got to spend with her son. If it wasn't too cold outside every afternoon she, Mason and Angel would take a family stroll around the neighborhood.

The memories they were creating as a family were ones she'd cherish forever. Dealing with her stomach and colostomy bag had become a lot easier too. Dylan now knew what foods to avoid because certain ones caused her to have diarrhea or become constipated. Her life was slowly getting back to normal. She had her best friend in her life again and she and Angel had tried having intercourse. The experience was a painful one but Dylan got through it.

As long as her man was pleased that was all she cared about. It was mid morning and Dylan was in the kitchen chopping up pieces of a banana for Mason to eat along with his cereal when the doorbell rang. She wasn't expecting any company so she couldn't imagine who would be at the gate. Dylan wiped her hands on a towel and went to the door.

"Who is it?" She asked through the intercom.

"State."

Shocked by the sound of his voice, Dylan allowed him to enter through the gate. The last conversation they had she'd made it clear that she wanted nothing to do with him. In a matter of minutes he was walking in the house and standing before her.

"What are you doing here?" She asked, looking him up and down.

"I've wanted to come check on you for months now but Billie said that wasn't a good idea."

"You should've listened to Billie because she was right." Dylan turned her back on him and switched back into the kitchen.

State followed her.

"You're old dude here?" He looked around.

"My father is dead but if you're referring to my husband; no he's not here but he'll be back soon. So I suggest you say what you got to say and jet." Dylan pulled a chair up to Mason's high chair and began to feed him.

"Damn he's gotten big." State took off his jacket.

"That's what toddlers do, they grow," Dylan shot sarcastically.

"Are you going to ever stop being mad at me? I miss my friend."

"I miss shitting through my ass but I've gotten over it." Dylan spat, wiping Mason's mouth with a napkin.

"Least you haven't lost you sense of humor," State pulled up a seat at the table. "How are you feeling?"

"Better. I'm just waiting on the phone call for my reversal surgery."

"That's what's up." State replied, happy for her. "Look, I'm sorry for not telling you about Billie when I found out ya'll were homegirls. That was fucked up. I should've told you the truth."

"Yeah, you should've but you didn't. All I care about at this point is you being a good father to my nephew. Kyrese deserves nothing but the best from you."

"And I'm giving him that. That's my dude right there," State smiled at the thought of his son. "All I want is for you to stop being mad at me."

Dylan shot State a look that could kill and rolled her eyes.

"Boy, I have been forgiven you." She cracked up laughing. "I just wanted to make you squirm a little bit."

"Damn, that's cold blooded." State let out a sigh of relief.

"Life is too short to be sitting up mad about shit. It is what it is. I've moved on and am happily married."

"Speaking of moving on. I know Billie hasn't told you yet but she and I are trying to work things out."

"I kind of figured that."

"Word? How you know?"

"Cause every time I bring your name up, Billie get's hella quiet," Dylan snickered. "What ya'll do is ya'll business. Just don't hurt her.

"I swear to god I'm not. I love her man."

"The funny thing about it is I actually believe you."
Dylan smiled as she heard the sound of the front door close.

"Oh shit! Angel's home," she panicked.

"Babe, who's car is that parked in the
driveway?"Angel asked, entering the kitchen.

As soon as he spotted State sitting at his kitchen
table, Angel lost his shit.

"What the fuck is this nigga doing in my house?"
He mean-mugged Dylan.

"You can chill out cuz. I just came by to check on
Dylan," State responded instead.

"Was I fucking talking to you? I was talking to my
wife!" Angel yelled, scaring Mason.

"Baby, calm down," Dylan stood up and caressed
his arm.

"Nah, fuck that!" He slapped her hand away. "I
don't want this nigga in my house."

"Yo Dylan, it was good seeing you. I'm glad you're
doing better but I'ma head out." State grabbed his jacket.

"No wait!" Dylan stopped him "Ya'll need to
squash this silly ass beef ya'll got. Angel baby, I know you
don't like State but babe he didn't cheat by his self. I was a
willing participate at the time. I've changed and he's
changed. He's your nephew's father. He's going to be

around. You two have to learn how to coexist. And State, Angel is my husband now. I love him and I respect him and I need you to respect him as well."

"I don't have nothing against you, bruh. I apologize for what went down. What we did was foul but Dylan's right. I have changed. I'm not that dude anymore," State revealed.

Angel steadied his breathing. Dylan was right. He had to let the anger and resentment towards State go. It wasn't getting him anywhere. All it was doing was festering and causing him to act out negatively. If Dylan becoming sick hadn't taught him anything it taught him that life was too short. None of them were promised tomorrow so it was best he spend his time on earth being happy. He and State would never be buddy-buddy but it was time to bury the hatchet.

"It's all good," Angel responded.

"Is it okay if State and I have supervised play dates every now and then?" Dylan crinkled her nose.

"Don't push it, Dylan," Angel ice grilled her.

Epilogue

A full year later, Dylan stood proudly in the back of the room watching closely as friends, family, bloggers and journalist sat quietly enjoying the first episode of her new web series called, Forever 21. After recovering from her reversal surgery and having her ovaries and fallopian tubes removed, Dylan made a vow to herself to live her life to the fullest. She was cancer free and she couldn't have anymore children but she had her son and her husband.

Dylan still wanted another child though. She and Angel had discussed adoption as an option but until they made a final decision, Dylan concentrated all of her energy on her upcoming web series Forever 21 and her new clothing line Pretty Ratchet Thingz. Dylan loved to bake but her first love was always fashion. The line debuted to great reviews and tons of sales. Her new Edible Couture location in New York was the number 1 bakery in Manhattan. Every morning there were lines wrapped around the building. Angel defended his world heavy weight title and won. He was now preparing for yet another bout with another opponent.

Dylan glanced over at Billie who was snuggled up next to State. State had kept his word and made an honest woman out of her. He and Billie were now married and she was pregnant with their second child. Billie being with State brought out the absolute best in her. She was way more at ease and didn't take life too seriously anymore. The two were meant to be with one another. They were soul mates.

Billie had everything she could've ever wanted. She had her man, her new baby on the way, her son and her girls back. After several delays, Billie finally had her day in court with Cain. The new judge heard both parties' and their witnesses sides and after careful consideration granted Billie back full custody of her girls. Cain tried appealing the judge's decision but the appeal was thrown out of court for lack of evidence.

Billie couldn't believe that Cain could be so petty and malicious as to appeal the ruling. State had to make her realize that some people were just never going to change. What mattered most was that Kyrese and State were closer than ever. The bond they shared was unbreakable. State constantly encouraged Kyrese and was a shoulder for him to lean on. Billie was no longer afraid to be herself. After years of putting it off she decided to give the music industry a shot and began working along side State at his record label. It was the best decision she'd made since taking him back.

All of her life Dylan was known as an air-head, a socialite, and a material girl. Her love of everything that glittered ruled her world but after becoming sick nothing about Dylan was the same. She'd changed. She was no longer the wide-eyed, naive girl that would sell her left leg for a Chanel bag. Yes, designer things were nice. They made her feel pretty and she enjoyed the compliments she got when wearing them. But none of those things mattered in the bigger scheme of things.

What mattered was being the best person she could be, being honest, giving back, spreading positivity and being true to herself. When she walked she now walked with a vengeance. Everything she did had a purpose. It took a while to figure out where she was going in life but not she was where she wanted to be. She was living in her truth. The sky was the limit for Dylan Dahl Monroe Carter. It was time to the show the world she was a big girl now. She was a grown ass woman and she could do whatever she wanted.

CPSIA information can be obtained at www.ICGtesting.com
Printed in the USA
LVOW04s1623310814

401739LV00018B/787/P